MULAN

Five Versions of a
Classic Chinese Legend
with Related Texts

MULAN

*Five Versions of a
Classic Chinese Legend
with Related Texts*

Edited and Translated,
with an Introduction,
by

Shiamin Kwa and
Wilt L. Idema

Hackett Publishing Company, Inc.
Indianapolis/Cambridge

Copyright © 2010 by Hackett Publishing Company, Inc.

19 18 17 16   2 3 4 5 6 7

For further information, please address:

    Hackett Publishing Company, Inc.
    P.O. Box 44937
    Indianapolis, IN 46244-0937

    www.hackettpublishing.com

Cover design by Abigail Coyle
Text design by Carrie Wagner
Composition by Agnew's, Inc.

Library of Congress Cataloging-in-Publication Data

Mulan shi. English
    Mulan : five versions of a classic Chinese legend with related texts / edited and
translated, with an introduction, by Shiamin Kwa and Wilt L. Idema.
      p. cm.
    Includes bibliographical references.
    ISBN 978-1-60384-196-2 (pbk.) — ISBN 978-1-60384-197-9 (cloth)
    I. Hua, Mulan (Legendary character)—Literary collections.   I. Kwa, Shiamin.
II. Idema, W. L. (Wilt L.)

    PL2668.M83.E13 2010
    895.1'124—dc22   2009035628

The paper used in this publication meets the minimum requirements
of American National Standard for Information Sciences—
Permanence of Paper for Printed Library Materials,
ANSI Z39.48–1984

CONTENTS

PREFACE

The exploits of Mulan, the legend of the White Snake, the romance of Liang Shanbo and Zhu Yingtai, and the thwarted love of Weaving Maiden and Buffalo Boy continue to fascinate Chinese audiences all over the world. As the embodiment of the wisdom, virtue, and pursuit of love of the Chinese people, these tales have been told and retold throughout the twentieth century; they have also been performed on the stage, adapted for the screen, and rewritten as dramas for television. They have inspired theme parks and postage stamps, violin concerti, and Western-style operas. In their modern transformations these traditional tales have been hailed as the quintessence of Chinese culture, as instruments for cultural renewal, and as tools of criticism.

The earliest extant premodern versions of these Chinese tales and legends are no less varied and multiform than their modern adaptations. By the time of recording, each of these stories had already undergone a centuries-long period of development and change. Depending on the time, region, and genre in which the version was created, each is unique and brings its own perspective and meaning to the story. Moreover, each of these texts reflects the idiosyncracies and personality of its author (whose name has usually been lost). We could make no greater mistake than to assume that these stories embody a single, unchanging, essential meaning, even though many modern and contemporary scholars write about these stories as if they do.

Despite the popularity of these tales with modern and contemporary authors and intellectuals, in premodern times these legends (with the exception of Mulan) were mostly ignored by the scholars and literati of late imperial China. They flourished in the realm of oral literature and in the many genres of traditional popular literature (*suwenxue*). This series aims to introduce the contemporary English reader to the richness and variety of the traditional Chinese popular literature of this period and to the wide discrepancies between the different adaptations of each story by translating at least two premodern adaptations in full. Each of these sets of translations will be preceded by an introduction tracing the historical development of each story up to the beginning of the twentieth century. The translations will be followed by a selection of related materials that will provide readers with a fuller understanding of the historical development of each story and will help them place the translated text in the development of Chinese popular literature and culture.

ACKNOWLEDGMENTS

The final version of this volume was made possible by the efforts and contributions of many others. The staff of the Harvard-Yenching Library provided assistance in locating obscure materials. An anonymous reader of the manuscript suggested an article that had previously escaped our notice. Maria Franca Sibau emailed corrections, images, and citations. Professor Wai-Yee Li at Harvard University meticulously combed through my Xu Wei translation to save me from a number of errors. Dr. Robert Roses read multiple drafts of the introduction for clarity, and offered a non-specialist's perspective. The hard work of the editorial and production staff at Hackett Publishing Company made the completion of this volume seem effortless from start to finish. Our editor, Rick Todhunter, oversaw this project with cheerful enthusiasm. Meera Dash, Carrie Wagner, Ruth Goodman, and the production staff meticulously combed through the text, uncovering errors and redundancies. All authors should be so lucky to work with such thoughtful and responsive people.

In spite of all their considerable efforts, and many more, all faults and errors of course remain completely my own.

Shiamin Kwa

INTRODUCTION

In the rich Chinese tradition of tales and legends that originated centuries ago and survives to this day, the story of Mulan, with its utter lack of supernatural demonstrations or interventions, is one of the most mundane. A heroine such as Meng Jiangnü successfully destroys the Great Wall with her tears of grief at news of her husband's death; the White Snake takes human form to pursue a worthy scholar and is punished for her vainglory with eternal imprisonment in Thunder Peak Pagoda; and the thwarted lovers Zhu Yingtai and Liang Shanbo are transformed into butterflies after their deaths, so that they can be together forever in lepidopterous love. In contrast, the subject of this volume, Mulan, simply puts on her father's armor and takes on a male identity to go to battle. Yet, the very feasibility of this action is what makes it so compelling, as well as revolutionary. Transformation is not about magic spells or divine intervention: it is about the deliberate and basic action of changing clothes.

Though the story of Mulan has been reiterated over the centuries, a few basic elements have remained constant. A young girl's elderly and sickly father is called up in the draft. The family knows that he is too ill to go, but they have no alternative: they have a daughter (sometimes two), but women are excluded from joining the all-male military, and a son, who is too young to enlist. The father decides that he has no option but to go. Mulan tells her parents that she will serve in his place. To do so, she will need to disguise herself as a man. She goes to the market to buy the necessities for travel and battle, dons her father's armor, and joins a group of young men heading off to war. For a dozen years, she fights side by side with them, preserving her chastity and hiding the fact that she is a woman from even her closest companions. She successfully leads a battle that decisively ends the war and is lauded by the emperor for her efforts. Instead of accepting an official post, she asks to return home to her parents. When she arrives, she returns to her old room, takes off her armor, puts on her dress and makeup, and effortlessly resumes her old life.

There have been variations in the story over the centuries, but they are comparatively minor ones. Different versions emphasize different motives. In some, Mulan is a filial daughter forced into the circumstances by her duty to her father; in others, Mulan is a fiercely patriotic fighter willing to risk her life for her country, where so few men will. Other versions add a romantic subplot: in Xu Wei's version, Mulan returns home and is promptly married to her next-door neighbor, Mr. Wang, and in the 1930s film version, a troubled attraction between Mulan and a fellow soldier is swiftly resolved when she dresses up as a woman again at the end. The basic structure remains unchanged: a girl becomes a man out of necessity, fulfills the task that required her to change, changes back once the goal is accomplished, and seeks to return to her former life. This matter-of-fact transition from one identity to another is fascinating, and it draws our attention to how much role-playing is a part of life. The multiplicity of identities occurs on multiple layers. Within the Mulan story, of course, we see directly how Mulan takes on and sheds personae according to the various demands of her circumstances. As we will see in the versions in this volume, the story takes different emphases, perhaps influenced by the biases of the author or the cultural climate at the time of its production. Readers, too, project their own particular interests onto Mulan.[1]

Because of this versatility, the legend of Mulan has endured for hundreds of years.[2] This is not to say that the legend's popularity has been consistent since its arrival. Indeed, there is no documentation to suggest that the recognition that Mulan enjoys in the twenty-first century is an unbroken continuation from her appearance in the "Poem of Mulan" more than a millennium ago. The story, as modified to represent Mulan as a Han Chinese loyalist battling an encroaching barbarian outsider, became a neat allegory for growing concerns about national identity and collaboration in the early twentieth century. Likewise, the Annie Oakley aspects of our heroine captured the attention of twentieth-century Chinese women looking for native independent female role models, and those in the West who looked eastward for strong female characters. In the last few decades alone, Maxine Hong Kingston appropriated parts of the Mulan story in her novel *The Woman Warrior*; Disney chose Mulan for its first Chinese heroine in a feature-length animated film; and, at the time of this book's writing, a new film version is in production by a Mainland Chinese studio, and another version is currently in development. Whatever the reasons, although Mulan may not have made much of an impression when she first arrived on the scene, she is now certainly the most recognized Chinese folktale heroine in the world.

---

[1] Joan Judge has chronicled the push and pull of Mulan as patriot versus Mulan as filial girl from the late-imperial period to the early twentieth century (2008, pp. 143–86).

[2] There is to our knowledge no evidence of a historical Mulan. Sanping Chen has argued, however, that the name "Mulan," which means "magnolia" in Chinese, is derived from a foreign word meaning "bull" or "stag," was a "style" or courtesy name adopted by military men in the fifth and sixth centuries, and was used as a surname by non-Han Chinese families (2005, pp. 23–43).

I. The "Poem of Mulan" and "Song of Mulan," from the Collected Works of the Music Bureau

The earliest recorded versions of the Mulan legend are two poems printed in the *Collected Works of the Music Bureau* (*Yuefu shiji*), an anthology compiled by Guo Maoqian in the twelfth century. The first work, "Poem of Mulan" ("Mulan shi"), is undated and anonymous, and it is followed by an imitation, translated in this volume as "Song of Mulan," written by the Tang dynasty official Wei Yuanfu (mid-eighth century). The "Poem of Mulan" contains details, such as the reference to the ruler by the term "khan," that suggest the northeastern conflicts of the Northern Wei period (386–533). Guo Maoqian claims that the poem is taken from the *Musical Records, Old and New* (*Gujin yuelu*), a text that is no longer extant and which dates from approximately the sixth century C.E.[3] This dating was adopted by Xu Wei (1521–1593) as the setting of his influential play, which further secured the tradition of dating the poem to that time, but there is no external corroborating evidence for an exact date of composition. Already in the twelfth century we see a disparity between the two earliest versions of the Mulan legend. The "Poem of Mulan" gives us a final stanza marveling at the difficulties of telling apart male from female, with the image of two hares running together; this image will recur in Xu Wei's play and in a 1939 film version. The "Song of Mulan" emphasizes Mulan's extraordinary demonstration of filial piety and loyalty.

The "Poem of Mulan" begins with the image of Mulan performing the typically female task of weaving while lamenting her situation:

> A sigh, a sigh, and then again a sigh—
> Mulan was sitting at the door and weaving.
> One did not hear the sound of loom and shuttle,
> One only heard her heave these heavy sighs.
> When she was asked the object of her love,
> When she was asked who occupied her thoughts,
> She did not have a man she was in love with,
> There was no boy who occupied her thoughts.
>
> "Last night I saw the summons from the army,
> The Khan is mobilizing all his troops.
> The list of summoned men comes in twelve copies:
> Every copy lists my father's name!"

---

[3] Wei, 1979, pp. 373–5.

Reasoning that her brother is too young to take their father's place, Mulan decides aloud that she will substitute for her father. She plans to get only a saddle and a horse, and there is no discussion about her change of clothes into male disguise:

> The eastern market: there she bought a horse;
> The western market: there she bought a saddle.
> The southern market: there she bought a bridle;
> The northern market: there she bought a whip.

Rather, the transformation into a man predominantly involves equipment, suggesting that it will be deeds that distinguish her. The ballad's emphases are subtle, but significant: in the middle section, details of Mulan's departure from home and her life as a soldier are expressed primarily through what is heard, whether it is the clacking of the shuttle, the girl's sighs, the wind's whistling, or the horses' whinnying. With the exception of the cold light on her armor, it is not so much what she sees that captures the emotion, but what she hears.

When Mulan returns home, she changes back into her female clothes. Here, the poem describes the removal of her soldier's garments and the steps she takes to return to her old self, moving from east to west in her chambers. Mulan takes off her soldier's buffcoat and puts on her skirt and makeup.

The ballad ends with the hare analogy appended as a sort of moral to the story, describing the surprised reactions of her fellow soldiers:

> "We marched together for these twelve long years
> And absolutely had no clue that Mulan was a girl!"
> "The male hare wildly kicks its feet;
> The female hare has shifty eyes,
> But when a pair of hares runs side by side,
> Who can distinguish whether I in fact am male or female?"

The analogy is an intriguing one: there are concrete ways of telling apart male and female. The hares have specific gendered characteristics, but these characteristics are obscured by the activity natural to animals with a nervous spring and wandering eyes: they are always in motion, and when they are in motion, those characteristics are hard to see. Men and women, unlike hares, do not have different eyes or legs. They do have natural physical differences, and sometimes, as will be emphasized in Xu Wei's play, culturally imposed physical differences like bound feet. These, too, can be obscured. Time and again, in Mulan's case, the human analogy for the evasive effect of hares running side by side is clothing. When hares run, their physical difference is obscured; when people are dressed identically, their sexual difference is obscured.

When Mulan dressed as a male, her brave actions and her assertions were accepted without question as a man's. Interestingly, it is female characteristics that are emphasized as being put on; little mention is made of dressing up as a man, with the exception of battle wear. As noted earlier, the transition into becoming a male soldier in the ballad is to get the appropriate equipment. Equipment is equally important in transforming a male civilian into a male soldier; the category is changed by clothing, but it is not a gender category. Sufen Lai writes about the contrast between the scenes of changing into a male and changing back into a female: "Such contrasting treatments in describing Mulan's transforming herself and assuming different roles suggest that women's cross-dressing was still a taboo subject even under the Confucian premise of filial piety; therefore, her transformation into a warrior is suggested with the purchasing of a gallant horse and its necessary gear, while her return to womanhood is detailed with feminine motions, objects and sentiments."[4] Lai convincingly argues that the ballad's audience would not have been as accepting of a woman's cross-dressing, but the conclusions reach beyond audience discomfort to suggest the possibility of a different way to read maleness and femaleness. Mulan had been introduced at the beginning of the ballad with the equipment of femaleness as well: the weaving shuttle that clicks its reminder of women's work. But when the soldier's buffcoat is taken off, and her hair is styled and makeup reapplied, it is not in response to a service or social role: she is putting on femaleness. Or, to put it the opposite way, femaleness is a kind of social role: it is an addition to the essential humanity of the male role. As the visual vocabulary and the hare metaphor seem to imply, gender, like a social role, is something that can be put on.

Wei Yuanfu's "Song of Mulan" is not significantly different from the "Poem of Mulan" in basic content, but it presents a different emphasis. The author was a prime minister in the Tang dynasty (618–907), during the Dali period (766–779) following the An Lushan and Shi Siming rebellion (755–763), which resulted in the near collapse and severe weakening of the Tang dynasty. Neighboring nations in Mongolia and Tibet saw their opportunities for advantage, and for a time (in the year 763) the Tang capital, Chang'an, was occupied by

---

[4] Sufen Sophia Lai, "From Cross-Dressing Daughter to Lady Knight-Errant: The Origin and Evolution of Chinese Women Warriors," *Presence and Presentation: Women in the Chinese Literati Tradition*, ed. Sherry Mou (New York: St. Martin's, 1999), p. 86.

Tibetan troops. Perhaps the contemporary circumstances weighed on Wei Yuanfu's mind, as he incorporates Tibetan incursions into his version of the Mulan legend.

The poem begins with the same justifications for Mulan's action ("My father has grown old, and worn by age; / How can he survive service?"). The "Song" provides the same details as the "Poem of Mulan," describing Mulan washing away the powder from her face and then later removing "turban and gauntlet" when she returns to her parents. While the "Poem of Mulan" draws attention to the difficulties of telling male from female, the "Song" makes this distinction a pointed argument:

> "Before, I was a hero among warriors,
> But from now on I'll be your darling girl again!"
> Relatives bring wine in congratulations:
> "Only now do we know that a daughter is as useful as a son!"

Mulan sings about her transformation back into her parents' "darling girl" just as celebrating neighbors draw attention to their newfound appreciation of daughters. We should not assume, however, that here Wei Yuanfu makes a protofeminist argument about equality; the comparison is not made to emphasize the equal qualities of women to men, but rather to demonstrate how one exceptional woman reveals the inadequacies of most men:

> If in this world the hearts of officials and sons
> Could display the same principled virtue as Mulan's,
> Their loyalty and filiality would be unbroken;
> Their fame would last through the ages—how could it be destroyed?

In the subtle variations from the "Poem of Mulan," a shift in emphasis results in a new reading. When the story regained momentum nearly five hundred years later, it would include even greater elaborations and interpretations.

II. The Female Mulan Joins the Army in Place of Her Father, *by Xu Wei*

The sixteenth-century play *The Female Mulan Joins the Army in Place of Her Father* (*Ci Mulan ti fu congjun*) was part of a quartet of plays called the *Four Cries of a Gibbon*

(*Sisheng yuan*) written by the late-Ming dynasty man of arts Xu Wei.[5] The *Four Cries of a Gibbon* are strikingly original comic plays that each elaborate on themes of identity, performance, disguise, and recognition. Xu Wei was famed for his talent in calligraphy, painting, and the literary arts, and he made his reputation with an unrestrained style that mirrored his eccentric life: his works of art sought to mimic spontaneous emotion rather than copy generic literary forms. As an artist and as a writer, he influenced later generations, who held him up as a model for the free and unrestricted individual style that they sought to emulate. The three plays that accompany *The Female Mulan* in the *Four Cries of a Gibbon* are all deeply invested in questions of who a person is and how that person portrays him- or herself to others.

After the two poems from the twelfth-century Music Bureau compilation previously discussed, there were no treatments of the story of Mulan until Xu Wei's version. Xu Wei's play, which introduced the surname Hua (meaning "flower") to our heroine, may be credited for resurrecting the story, which became the popular subject of novel and play adaptations in the centuries that followed, up to this day. The play is concerned not with issues of historical accuracy but with entertainment: how did this girl carry out her transformation and how did she sustain her deception for a dozen years? Although there is unfortunately no documentation of performances of *The Female Mulan*, stage directions and the play itself allow one to easily imagine a performance that takes advantage of costume changes, including a scene of Mulan unwinding her foot bandages as part of her transformation into a man, staged battle scenes, and accompanying descriptive songs.

The play is divided into two acts. The first act begins with the protagonist, played by a young female lead (*dan*) introducing herself as Hua Mulan, and provides the setting of the play, among the Xianbei tribe in the Northern Wei. Mulan notes that all men of age are being conscripted to subdue the rebellion of a fictional bandit leader named Leopard Skin. Concerned that her father is too elderly to serve, Mulan decides to take his place. This decision is followed by an offstage shopping excursion that launches a series of songs about the various

---

[5] The reader should be reminded that until the twentieth century, what we call a "play" in Chinese literature was actually a sung drama, more akin to a Western opera or Broadway musical, with alternation between arias set to existing tunes, and recited speeches, than to spoken-word plays. *The Female Mulan* is a *zaju*, a short dramatic form of four or five acts from the Yuan dynasty (1279–1368). By the time *The Female Mulan* was written in the late Ming dynasty, the genre rules were significantly loosened: the plays of *Four Cries of a Gibbon* range in length from one to five acts.

accessories she buys. The middle of the act is taken up with stage work, accompanied by descriptive songs. In the third aria, Mulan removes her footbindings. Although bound feet are anachronistic for a woman of the Northern Wei, a setting deliberately chosen by Xu Wei, the opportunity for such a scene must have been irresistible. One can easily imagine the titillating entertainment value of this action, and its potential for visual comedy. Mulan changes her feet back "into floating boats" (large, natural feet) but assures the audience that she will be able to return them to their golden lotus glory with the help of a secret family recipe. Having treated the audience to a "foot show," she commences to change her costume, from her women's clothes into soldier's clothing. She demonstrates a soldier's skill by performing martial arts with sword, staff, and bow and arrow, one after the other. She receives her parents' blessings and leaves with two fellow soldiers, in search of Leopard Skin's lair.

Act 2 begins in the heat of battle, with the commanding general, Xin Ping, employing "Hua Hu" (Mulan) to lead the raid on Leopard Skin. They successfully invade the bandit hideout and capture Leopard Skin. Hua Hu is singled out for his part in the capture and is given cap and girdle as symbols of a promotion to a position in the Imperial Secretariat. Hua Hu is thus sent home, still as a man, in the company of her two fellow soldiers, to await the new appointment. Hua Hu sings an aria about how the one who captured the bandit king was a fraud and therefore that the successes were not due to *her* work. As she travels with the soldiers, they comment on how strange it is that they have never seen Hua Hu use the toilet. "Hua Hu" mysteriously tells them about a statue in his village whose face changed to that of Chang'e.[6] Returning home, "Hua Hu" first reapplies female makeup, then greets her family. She shares her successes with her parents, showing them the cap and girdle she has been granted, and then confirms that she returns to them as a "dogwood bud," or virgin. After her amazed fellow soldiers leave, a young male lead (*sheng*) also wearing cap and girdle enters; he is Mr. Wang, the neighbor's son who has succeeded in the exams. The two have been conveniently matched by their parents and are immediately married on stage. The wedding is also one of Xu Wei's innovations to the inherited Mulan tradition. Luo Qiuzhao suggests that this reflects the influence of Ming dynasty plays, which conventionally end with a reunion scene or wedding.[7] If Mulan cannot keep the cap and girdle, at least she ought to be married to one who can.

---

[6] The goddess of the moon.

[7] Luo, 1996, p. 76.

The play ends with Mulan singing the following song, which quotes the end of the "Poem of Mulan":

> I was a woman till I was seventeen,
> Was a man for twelve more years.
> Passed under thousands of glances,
> Which of them could tell cock from hen?
> Only now do I believe that a distinction between male
> and female isn't told by the eyes.
> Who was it really occupied Black Mountain Top?
> The girl Mulan went to war for her pop.
> The affairs of the world are all such a mess,
> Muddling boy and girl is what this play does best.

Discussions of Xu Wei's play have aligned with the readings of the ballad and do not make much of their differences; those scholars who do discuss the theme of cross-dressing in *The Female Mulan* mainly discuss either the terms of its place in the literary tradition, its incipient feminism in Xu Wei's work, or its acquiescence to the patriarchy with Mulan's return to womanhood and domesticity at the end. Written a few decades before the spectacularly traumatic end of the Ming dynasty, *The Female Mulan* does not make use of the female figure as a critique of the ineffectual male who could not act appropriately in service of his country. The transgressions in *The Female Mulan* are not really that transgressive: Mulan uses expedient means to carry out a task and, having succeeded, seems to return to exactly who she was when she began. Something strange occurs in this play; what is most affecting is not the obvious fact of the switching from female to male and then back again, but rather the complete disavowal of its strangeness. Xu Wei's play, for all its apparent superficiality and inadequacies, does propose some fascinating questions about the performance of the self.

The Female Mulan engages questions of gender in a much more complicated manner than the "Poem of Mulan." The play clearly presents a case of performance, and a performance that is crucial both domestically and nationally to Mulan; yet, the character who carries out that performance dismisses her actions completely. Mulan uses the strategies of costume and speech to create a self, mocks the belief that sight can be trusted, and leaves the audience with a conundrum when considering the entire performance. If actions in battle scenes were as if performed by someone else, to whom do we direct our appreciation? Similarly, in watching a play, what constitutes our experience of what happens onstage? Does acting nullify all actions performed under cover of disguise? *The Female Mulan* suggests that questions of gender or loyalty are not primary considerations. Rather, the play points to more profound questions about how we define ourselves in general: aren't we all simply playing parts? If we are, how do we keep hold of our "true" selves?

III. Mulan in Drama and Prose in the Qing Dynasty

After Xu Wei, adaptations of the legend of Mulan proliferated during the Qing dynasty (1644–1911). The non-Han Chinese Manchus, neighbors from the north, established the Qing dynasty, which replaced centuries of consecutive Han Chinese rule during the Ming. This change of regime, emphasized by marked changes in language, costume, and hairstyle, among other things, appears to have had some effect on the Mulan version we encounter during this period. Whereas Xu Wei took liberties with historical detail for the sake of entertainment, making up a bandit king named Leopard Skin as the enemy and inserting anachronous footbinding for dramatic effect (and titillation), these later versions returned to emphasizing filial piety and patriotism, this time with a specifically ethnic cast to the story. With Mulan, the writers found an opportunity to present a heroine who embodied their vaunted qualities of loyalty to a ruler against an invading, outside force. Summaries of the lengthy Mulan plays and novels of this period are supplied in the appendixes at the end of this volume.

We see here the preoccupations with emphasizing chastity and loyalty, with the trope of suicide. In contrast to the previous versions we have encountered, here Mulan is driven to committing suicide to express the pureness of her heart. Winning battles and coming home unscathed and virginal are no longer heroic enough. The widely popular hundred-chapter *Historical Romance of the Sui and Tang* (*Sui Tang yanyi*; c. 1675), compiled by Chu Renhuo (c. 1630–c. 1705), includes a version of the legend of Mulan in chapters 55 through 61 (see Appendix 2). The action of the story is set during the final years of the Sui dynasty (581–618 C.E.), when rebellions had broken out all over China, and the Turks had joined in the warfare. Mulan is portrayed as the daughter of a Turkish father and a Chinese mother; when the khan conscripts her father, Mulan goes in his place. The familiar elements of the story are expanded with many secondary characters, including the formidable woman warrior Dou Xianniang who first captures Mulan but later comes to admire her and take her on as a personal attendant. At the novel's end, the defeated but pardoned Mulan returns home to find that her father has died and that the khan wants to take her into his harem.

Rather than submit, Mulan commits suicide, entrusting her sister to carry out a mission in male dress. In *The Story of the Loyal, Filial, and Heroic Mulan* (*Zhongxiao yonglie Mulan zhuan*), likely dating from some time in the late eighteenth century, the action is set somewhat later, beginning with the end of the Sui and taking place during the reign of Tang Taizong (599–649) (Appendix 2). In this novel, Mulan is now surnamed Zhu and is a Chinese maiden from Hubei. In this lengthier version, Zhu Mulan is given three generations of back story. The novel also inserts many supernatural elements, such as mystical and secret fighting techniques given to Mulan's grandfather, Zhu Ruoxu. Mulan learns the doctrines and techniques at her grandfather's knee and receives all his books when he dies. Mulan continues to train in the arts of warfare, in addition to the feminine arts of spinning and weaving, and successfully defeats a fox spirit who reappears to challenge Mulan again in battle. Eventually, Mulan triumphs and is rewarded with titles. When she reveals that she is a woman, Taizong makes her a princess, and she returns home to raise her now orphaned brothers. Taizong repeatedly entreats Mulan to return to the capital, but she respectfully refuses in order to stay at home to care for her brothers. Eventually, Taizong falls prey to gossip and summons Mulan for a third time, with the intent of murder. This time Mulan again refuses and underscores her sincerity by committing suicide. Taizong, overwhelmed with remorse, constructs monuments in Mulan's memory, and she is later given a posthumous title. As in the *Historical Romance of the Sui and Tang*, Mulan has to go to the extremes of suicide to make her mark in history.

In the eighteenth century, we see an expansion of *The Female Mulan* by Xu Wei into a forty-scene *chuanqi* by the Manchu prince Yong'en (1727–1805), who gave his play the title *A Couple of Hares* (*Shuangtu ji*) and opted to keep the happier ending of a wedding (Appendix 1). As a member of the Manchu aristocracy, Yong'en may well have found the Northern Wei a convenient historical parallel to the Qing dynasty. His play can be read as a celebration of Han Chinese loyalty to their Manchu rulers. Yong'en had to come up with many new characters and episodes in order to fill his forty scenes, and, to conform to the conventions of *chuanqi*, he greatly expanded the role of Mulan's fiancé from childhood, now given the full name of Wang Qingyun. He also gave Leopard Skin a younger sister, who falls in love with Mulan and is willing to betray her brother for the opportunity to marry the handsome enemy officer. In the play we are also treated, as we are in the expanded novelizations, to supernatural intervention, although again not in Mulan's case. Her special skills are mundanely earned, but they are powerful enough to either inspire supernatural occurrences or else defeat them. In this case, the apparition of Guanyin (a female manifestation of an originally male bodhisattva) comes and goes, reminding the viewer that shape and identity shifting is a key element in Mulan's successes. Yong'en's play may have had some impact on the way Mulan was portrayed on the Peking opera stage of the twentieth century, which continued to use the Northern Wei for its setting. It also provided Mulan with impassioned speeches about the exceptional behavior that she commits as a woman, delivered as a challenge to all men. Here, rather than posing as her father, Mulan identifies herself as Hua Hu's son, also going by the name Hua Hu, a variation that recurs in some of the later adaptations. The actual scenes of battle are engaged with some detail here, with introductions to Xin Ping, the commander in chief, and Niu He, the unworthy and lecherous superior who lusts after "Hua Hu" and fails miserably in battle. Here, too, Yong'en inserts other memorable characters, including the bandit king's stepsister, who falls in love with "Hua Hu" and agrees to defect. The play ends happily with Mulan taking her leave to return home to her village, where her parents are ennobled and her fiancé receives a title. On her way home, Mulan again sees her childhood pets, a pair of rabbits running toward her, and she changes back into female dress to her companions' surprise.

Yong'en's play appears to have been the direct source for one more vernacular novel, *An Extraordinary History of the Northern Wei: The Story of a Filial and Heroic Girl* (*Bei Wei qishi guixiao*; 1850) by Zhang Shaoxian (Appendix 2), which appeared as the Manchu Qing was beset by foreign and internal foes, when models of filial piety and loyalty to a barbarian dynasty were in short supply. The forty-six-chapter novel, like the *Historical Romance of the Sui and Tang* and *The Story of the Loyal, Filial, and Heroic Mulan*, takes advantage of the length allowed by novels to expand the story. Unlike the other two novels, the Mulan story here is, true to Yong'en and Xu Wei, returned to the Northern Wei. The story adds political intrigue and the infighting that occurs even between members of the same side: Mulan is betrayed by her superior, Niu He, who jealously refuses to acknowledge her achievements to the generalissimo Xin Ping. This novelization also introduces other female characters: Lu Wanhua, a concubine who becomes a sworn sister; and the bandit leader's wife, Miao Fengxian, who is a formidable warrior finally defeated by Mulan. Mulan fights side by side with her former concubine and sworn sister, Lu Wanhua, and successfully defeats the bandits. Mulan and Wanhua have sworn to marry Mulan's childhood sweetheart, Wang Qingyun, and the novel is ended with a celebratory wedding with titles distributed all around. To allay any remaining doubts about Mulan's commitment to her female duties, the consummation of the wedding is also described.

In the final years of the Qing dynasty, as China faced increasing pressure from imperialist powers, playwrights turned again to Mulan. The first scenes of *Hua*

Mulan, a *chuanqi* play in sixteen scenes by Chen Xu (1879–1940), were published as early as 1897 (Appendix I). More scenes followed later, but its first complete printing was not until 1914. Interestingly, the changing character of Mulan in this play seems to reflect its long gestation period. In the opening scenes, Mulan is still depicted as the perfect filial daughter who supports her aged and sickly father by her diligent weaving. As in Yong'en's play, Mulan goes to war as Hua Hu's son. By the end of the play, Mulan, supported by "good fellows from the green forests," is fighting foreign foes and swears not to come home before she will have defeated these barbarians for good. If the opening scenes reflect a traditional morality and seem to present Mulan once again as an example of filial piety and loyalty, the final scenes seem more inspired by the events of the Revolution of 1911. Indeed, as we shall see, Mulan's references to her political action become more strident as she enters the early twentieth century.

IV. Mulan as Opera: Mu Lan Joins the Army[8] *and Beyond*

By the time of *Mu Lan Joins the Army* (*Mu Lan congjun*), a Peking opera script first published in 1903, the emphasis on Mulan's patriotism had come to the forefront: the filial daughter has been clearly transformed into a feminist patriot. No author is mentioned, and none has been identified in later scholarship. The genre of the text is not specified either, but in view of its structure, the text was most likely intended to be performed as a Peking opera.[9] Unfortunately, there is no information on the performance history of the play, if there ever was any.[10] One can easily imagine, however, *Mu Lan Joins the Army* as a very lively play

---

[8] In most other accounts of the legend of Mulan of the Ming and Qing dynasties, the name "Mulan" is treated as a single word, and Mulan is provided with a surname, either Hua or Zhu. In this play, however, it appears that the syllable *mu* is treated as a surname "Mu." For instance, in speaking to Huo Qubing, Mu Lan often refers to herself as "Mu *lang*," which literally means "a young man surnamed Mu." For this reason, the name of the heroine of the play is transliterated here as Mu Lan.

[9] Yan Quanyi mentions *Mu Lan Joins the Army* as one of the earliest examples of reformist Peking opera, in his *Qingdai jingju wenxue shi* (2005, p. 439). Also see *Zhongguo jingju shi, shang juan,* 2005, p. 325.

[10] For instance, there are no references to *Mu Lan Joins the Army* in Wang Zhizhang, *Zhongguo jingju biannian shi,* 2 vols. (Beijing: Zhongguo xiju chubanshe, 2002), for the final years of the Qing.

in performance, and the stage directions make clear that our anonymous author very much wrote it with the intent of performance.

The action of the play is moved to the reign of Emperor Wu (r. 140–87 B.C.E.) of the Han dynasty, who pursued a policy of aggressive expansion in Mongolia and Central Asia with the aid of generals such as Huo Qubing and Wei Qing. This struggle between the Han and the Xiongnu (in earlier scholarship often identified with the Huns) is portrayed as the righteous war of the Chinese against the barbarians, who are chased back by Mu Lan and Wei Qing as far as the Northern Ice Sea. In the first part of the play, Mu Lan eagerly jumps at the opportunity to join the army once her cousin, despite his devotion to the martial arts, turns out to be too much of a coward to do his duty. Her primary motivation now is not filial piety, but "to shame those men" and to serve as a model for women. She is not shown weaving at all, and to the extent that filial piety is mentioned, it is only as an afterthought. In the second part, Mu Lan is ordered to meet up with Wei Qing and arrives just in time to save the general from an imminent defeat at the hands of the Xiongnu.[11] A note in the text points out that Wei Qing's distress has to be highlighted in order to stress the main theme of the play. At the end of the second part, Mu Lan explicitly declares that her actions have not been inspired by loyalty to a single person or a single dynasty, but by concern for the nation and the race. Pointedly, the play does not depict her return home.

The characterization of Mulan as a female patriot, or perhaps even a feminist patriot, was very much in tune with the times. As the political situation of China rapidly deteriorated following its defeat by Japan in 1895, Han Chinese turned more and more against the Manchus. At the same time, China's treatment of its women came increasingly to be seen as one of the major causes of its backwardness; this same period witnessed the rise of a strident feminism, which hailed Mulan (often compared to Joan of Arc) as one of the native models for the new Chinese woman, who would participate on equal footing with male citizens in building a new and strong nation. Patriots and feminists, both male and female, changed the meaning of the Mulan legend "from filiality to fearlessness, from a dutiful daughter's return home to an ethnic Han nationalist's heroic struggle against threatening foreign—read Manchu—forces."[12] Many

---

[11] All Chinese readers of the play probably will be reminded of the story of Li Ling, who failed to meet up with his commander, bravely fought the Xiongnu, but eventually, when outnumbered, surrendered to them.

[12] Judge, 2008, p. 143. Judge's comments are in particular inspired by a commentary on Mulan by Xu Dingyi in 1906. She discusses the various interpretations of the character of Mulan during the final decade of the Qing in more detail on pp. 151–162 of her study.

Photograph of Qiu Jin in contemporary Chinese male dress.

career women who grew up in the early decades of the twentieth century have testified to the enormous influence the model of a modernized Mulan exerted on them.[13] The debates on the future of China were not limited to the printed page but rather moved onto the stage. The theater, especially the Peking opera of Beijing and Shanghai, was very much a part, if not a driving force, of the intellectual ferment of the times.[14]

The overlap of history with a literary model is best expressed in the case of Qiu Jin (1875–1907). In 1904, the youngest daughter of a well-to-do family left her husband and young children to go to Japan, where she studied fencing

[13] Wang, 1999.

[14] Goldstein, 2007, esp. ch. 3, "The Experimental Stage" (pp. 89–133).

Photograph of Qiu Jin as a Japanese woman warrior, complete with sword.

and archery and experimented with various styles of dress, using Mulan as her role model. Qiu Jin is celebrated to this day as one of the first martyrs of the revolution against the Qing imperial government; upon returning from Japan, she edited a newspaper on women's issues and taught at a school in her native Zhejiang. In 1907, she attempted an uprising against the Qing but was captured and summarily executed. Qiu Jin's interest in the sartorial creation of her identity is evident in the photographic history she left behind: she alternatively appears in Japanese women's dress (specifically, that of a Japanese woman warrior, with sword drawn), Manchu male dress, and Western male dress. Her patriotic poems seek to emulate Mulan's example, as they are insistently nostalgic for a Han era before the entrance of the "barbarian" Manchus. Qiu Jin became an outspoken opponent of footbinding, that corporeal marker of gender that Xu Wei's

Mulan dismisses and regains with ease. The resonances between the real-life revolutionary who poses in various (and often male) costume and the literary heroine whose abilities are released by changes of clothes are nearly too perfect.[15]

Both cases demonstrate how easily identities could be tried on and discarded at will; a persona could be put on just as simply as a costume. Both cases also demonstrate the consequences of that ease; what remains underneath when so much ends up being surface? Does a body matter? When Qiu Jin was surrounded by Manchu troops and captured for treason in 1907, she reportedly refused to speak. She was then given a brush in order to write her confession. She wrote instead: "Autumn rain and autumn wind: the sorrow kills one." Qiu Jin plays on her surname, Qiu, which also means autumn, in these final, unspoken words. Instead of speaking her words, she wrote them down. Instead of inscribing her confession, she inscribed her biography. Instead of writing her life story, she took her life and made it into lyric.

Mulan's popularity endured and increased in the early twentieth century; her character was one of the roles taken on by the immensely popular and celebrated Peking opera star Mei Lanfang (1894–1961) in 1917. Mei was a world-famous star, who specialized in the role of the *dan*, or young female lead. The fact that he was a female impersonator was hardly atypical for an actor in Peking opera, but it lent itself to Mei's argument for equality between the sexes. Mulan's strength is contrasted with that of all the people of the country, not just women, and the blurring of gender is emphasized by the fact that this woman impersonating a man is played by Mei, a man impersonating a woman.[16]

In the 1917 interpretation of *Mulan Joins the Army* (Appendix I), cowritten with Qi Rushan, Mei chose the patriotic Mulan over the virtuous and filial Mulan. Here again, Mulan was to take on a symbolic role of patriot. The emphasis here is on the significance of political action, made especially heroic by the fact that it is carried out by a woman. The script emphasizes that it is a natural duty—and one not restricted by gender—to act on behalf of one's state. One's motives should not be personal but rather should consider the state's best interest; if the state were to collapse, private relationships would not be able to exist, either. The undated text for *On Campaign in Place of Her Father* (Appendix I), an alternative title for the Mei and Qi collaboration, focuses more on the additional character He Tingyu, who is the commander in chief of Hua Hu (really Mulan in her father's guise). The emphasis here is on military strategies and

---

[15] For more on Qiu Jin and her work, consult Idema and Grant, 2004, pp. 767–808.

[16] While Mei's performance of Mulan was quite a success, he would prefer in following years to portray female warriors who fought as women.

specific battles, but the resolution is the same: Mulan is heroic in battle but does not accept any appointments, choosing instead to return home to her life as a woman. Several other plays followed this one, continuing to emphasize the theme of women shaming men into accepting their political duty. In Pifu's one-act play, *Joining the Army: On the Road* (Appendix I), Mulan declares: "Since ancient times those who live in the inner compartments would not leave the gate, but how can the past be a model for the present, now that the country is in chaos?"

Mei took advantage of his role as an actor to demonstrate onstage how Mulan's gender switching emphasized the importance of political action: by making the actions of valor more important than whether they were performed by a man or a woman, Mei implicated every citizen in civic duty.[17] Offstage as well, he employed gender difference to express political objection. He pointedly withdrew from performing in Mainland China during the Japanese occupation. One of his ways of marking this protest was to grow a beard, physically emphasizing his gender and thus eradicating the female persona that was essential for his métier.

V. *The Film* Mulan Joins the Army

The 1939 film *Mulan Joins the Army* was produced by Zhang Shankun for Shanghai's Xinhua Film Company during the Japanese occupation, when most of the film world had fled to Hong Kong. Written by the playwright Ouyang Yuqian, directed by Bu Wancang, and starring the actress Chen Yunshang (Nancy Chan) in the title role, this film ran for a record-breaking eighty-three days beginning on the first day of the Chinese lunar year. Chen Yunshang was an instant hit. Her public identity was promoted as a contrasting alternative to other popular film actresses of the day; she was a thoroughly "modern" girl: athletic, vital, and "Western." This film, released in a Shanghai that was besieged by rivalries between Nationalist agents and agents of puppet regimes supported by the Japanese, tapped into the popular anxieties about occupation, collaboration, and domination.[18] *Mulan Joins the Army* is a thinly veiled allegory for the cause of resistance

---

[17] In an interesting gender twist, during the 1930s in occupied Shanghai, Mulan was a popular subject for the all-female casts of Zhejiang-style Yue "opera play" (*yueju*) performances. Jin Jiang writes about the opera play *Hua Mulan* as the first patriotic play of that type, one version an adaptation of Mei Lanfang's Peking opera. See Jiang, 2009, pp. 92–5.

[18] On this topic, consult Poshek Fu's *Between Shanghai and Hong Kong: The Politics of Chinese Cinemas* (2003). The book is a detailed study of the historical period and the role of films, and this film in particular, in addressing these anxieties.

in the name of national pride and love of country. Ouyang also rewrote the play in 1942 as a Guilin-style opera (*Guiju*); it has some modifications and omissions that appear to have been made to adapt to the different performance requirements of a staged rather than a film version (it is summarized in Appendix I).

The Mulan of *Mulan Joins the Army* is a patriotic heroine whose filial actions are only an extension of her profound sense of duty to her country. Mulan repeatedly scolds fellow soldiers for failing to unite against the barbarian enemy, and she comes against obstacles in the military leadership: she discovers that her leader is being led astray by an adviser who collaborates with the enemy. Undeterred, Mulan does her best to protect the leader while leading the troops to success against the foreigners. The film ends with Mulan declining the emperor's rewards and returning home to her parents where she reveals that she is a woman to her army companion. The two of them are united in marriage.

The film balances the weightier task of political criticism with the comic elements of Mulan's situation. Scenes make light of the differences in gender, often emphasizing how much gender is a performance. In one memorable scene, Mulan and Liu Yuandu go on a secret mission to explore enemy terrain; they not only travel in mufti, but Mulan dresses as a woman, encouraged to do so because "he" is already feminine. There is a lot of flirtation between Mulan and Liu Yuandu, even as Mulan is perceived to be a man, making for comedy to an audience that knows Mulan is a woman. The comedy serves to underscore the political allegory, however; how is it that this woman is the most successful soldier in the battalion? What is the matter with Chinese men?

Mulan Joins the Army opens with a scene that recalls the "Poem of Mulan" and *The Female Mulan*. We see Mulan in a hunting costume on horseback with bow and arrow, shooting and retrieving birds. She then sets her sights on a rustling in the bushes:

(*... From among some bushes, there is a rustling, and Mulan draws her bow and shoots at it. Striking her target, she suddenly hears a cry of pain. It is in fact another hunter who had been concealed in the bushes. In pain he jumps up, sees Mulan, and recognizes her.*)

LI: Wang, what were you calling out about again? Did you shoot something?

WANG: No, I didn't shoot anything; instead, I got shot by someone! Take a look . . .

(*He demonstrates to them where he was hit*)

ZHANG: Hey, isn't that a daughter of the Hua family?

(*Mulan rides over to the group*)

LI: That's right!

ZHANG: Pretending to be mad but actually scheming, she's come over to our village to hunt—and flaunt the rules!

LI: That's right!

MULAN: Big Brother Wang, I am truly sorry. I thought you were a rabbit. I didn't think you would have been crouching there.

We are returned here to the now centuries-old comparison of telling apart the male and female hare. Mulan mistakes Wang for a rabbit in the bushes, insulting him on multiple levels. Not only has she mistaken a man for an animal and struck him with an arrow, she tells him that she has mistaken him for a rabbit. By comparing him to a rabbit in particular, contemporary slang for a homosexual, she impugns his masculinity. Of course, this is the subtext of *Mulan Joins the Army*. Mulan is more "masculine" than any of the young braves in the film, inasmuch as masculinity is defined by courage, loyalty, and fearlessness in battle. Certainly, the young men of the village are portrayed as hapless and ineffectual, and neither Wang nor his shooting companions go off to battle at all.

In the country's time of need, it is only Mulan who can step forward to do what is right for her compatriots. Unthreatened by foreign incursion, unswayed by selfish greed, she outperforms the men. Yet, her exceptional behavior is simply that: exceptional. She stands out, but only as a role model, a symbol of what every *man* should strive to be. Once she has proven her potential, and demonstrated what can be accomplished with the right motives, she quickly steps down from present and future positions of power and marries the man who had been her subordinate throughout the many years of war: all's well that ends well. Mulan is ultimately not a role model to women, who are expected to stay at home to serve the family as her sister does, but a role model to men.

VI. Conclusion

Through the twentieth century into the twenty-first, the story of Mulan gained momentum, and it was adapted in opera and film versions over the decades. We have, for example, versions of Mulan written after the formation of the People's Republic of China in 1949 that make her a native of Yan'an, birthplace of Communist heroes. Mulan was a popular figure in Hong Kong films as well, especially in Cantonese-style Yue opera versions. She is called "Fa Muk Lan" according to Cantonese pronunciation and was a popular hit in the 1964 Cantonese opera film titled *Lady General Hua Mulan (Fa Muk Lan)*.

It is this Cantonese pronunciation of Mulan's surname that came to the English-speaking general audience when Maxine Hong Kingston published her novel *The Woman Warrior: A Girlhood among Ghosts* in 1989. Kingston took liberties with the Mulan legend, weaving into her interpretation threads of other stories and legends that she said were learned from hearing her mother's stories. Kingston's Fa Mu Lan was a critique of the oppression Kingston herself felt as a Chinese-American woman, and one of the reminders of that oppression to the protagonist is a series of grievances tattooed onto her back by her parents (a reference to the male hero Yue Fei). The narrator girds the memory of this fierce warrior, who is braver than any man, against the reality of her girlhood in San Francisco's Chinatown, where she finds herself being belittled for the fact that she is a girl. The novel uses the figure of Mulan to voice the grievances of a Chinese-American girl who grows up hearing the tales of a fierce role model but is expected to live out traditional roles. Instead of viewing the novel as a personal rumination on one girl's crises of identity set against a pastiche of partially observed notions of handed-down ethnicity, the Asian-American author and activist Frank Chin furiously objected to what he perceived as Kingston's re-Orientalizing of China to pander to a white audience. Kingston's best seller became, to Chin, a deliberate corruption of the Mulan legend for the sake of selling women's oppression in traditional China. Mulan resurfaced again in the 1990s, with the 1998 Disney animated movie *Mulan*, the first Chinese story to receive the Disney treatment. This Mulan was generally well received, and it plays the most significant role in Mulan's name recognition to popular audiences in the West.[19]

In recent years, Mulan has continued to be a popular subject for Chinese plays and films, both in Mainland China and in Hong Kong and Taiwan. In 2003, Li Liuyi produced an avant-garde stage adaptation of *Hua Mulan*. In 2008, a hybrid "Chinese opera" version of Mulan debuted at the Vienna State Opera House with music by Guan Xia played by the Vienna Symphony Orchestra. At the time of this book's writing, a film of Mulan starring Zhao Wei as the lead is currently in production.

Over the last millennium, Mulan has been transformed in the hands of writers and directors, as much as she transformed herself. Mulan's superiority as a

---

[19] See Lan, 2003.

woman committing acts of daring beyond the abilities of men, morally or martially, should not be immediately interpreted as evidence of a willingness to valorize women over men, however. The reader must consider that arguing for Mulan's moral superiority—preserving her chastity while defying expectations in filial or national gestures—may just be another way of arguing for the necessity of keeping her contained within the safe and protected confines of the domestic sphere. Though the interpretations and variations of the legend of Mulan may differ, Mulan herself endures: she is, after all, no stranger to change.

MULAN

ANONYMOUS

"Poem of Mulan"

A sigh, a sigh, and then again a sigh—
Mulan was sitting at the door and weaving.
One did not hear the sound of loom and shuttle,
One only heard her heave these heavy sighs.
 When she was asked the object of her love,
When she was asked who occupied her thoughts,
She did not have a man she was in love with,
There was no boy who occupied her thoughts.

"Last night I saw the summons from the army,
The Khan is mobilizing all his troops.
The list of summoned men comes in twelve copies:
Every copy lists my father's name!
 My father has, alas, no grown-up son,
And I, Mulan, I have no adult brother.
I want to buy a saddle and a horse,
To take my father's place and join the army."

The eastern market: there she bought a horse;
The western market: there she bought a saddle.
The southern market: there she bought a bridle;
The northern market: there she bought a whip.
 At dawn she said good-bye to her dear parents,
At night she rested by the Yellow River.
She did not hear her parents' voices, calling for their daughter,
She only heard the Yellow River's flowing water, always splashing, splashing.

At dawn she left the Yellow River's bank;
At night she rested on Black Mountain's top.
She did not hear her parents' voices, calling for their daughter,
She only heard the whinnying of Crimson Mountain's Hunnish[1] horsemen.

---

[1] The Chinese term *hu*, which we here translate as "Hunnish," generally refers to the nomadic populations on China's traditional nothern border (in modern Inner Mongolia).

Myriads of miles: she joined the thick of battle,
Crossing the mountain passes as if flying.
Winds from the north transmitted metal rattles,[2]
A freezing light shone on her iron armor.
A hundred battles and the brass were dead;
After ten years the bravest men returned.

When they returned, they met the Son of Heaven,
The Son of Heaven seated on his throne.[3]
Their honorary rank went up twelve steps,
And their rewards were counted in the millions.
    The Khan asked Mulan what he might desire—
"I, Mulan, do not care for an appointment here at court.[4]
Give me your racer good for a thousand miles,[5]
To take me back again to my old hometown."

Hearing their daughter had arrived, her parents
Went out the city, welcoming her back home.
Hearing her elder sister had arrived, her sister
Put on her bright red outfit at the door.
Hearing his elder sister had arrived, her brother
Sharpened his knife that brightly flashed in front of pigs and sheep.

"Open the gate to my pavilion on the east,
Let me sit down in my old western room.
I will take off the dress I wore in battle;
I will put on the skirt I used to wear."
    Close to the window she did up her hair;
Facing the mirror she applied makeup.
She went outside and saw her army buddies—

---

[2] The Chinese commentators here explain the "rattle" as a small iron three-legged pot, which was used for cooking food at daytime and for beating out the watches during nighttime.

[3] The Son of Heaven (the emperor/khan) is said in the original to be seated in the Hall of Light, a ceremonial structure described in ancient books.

[4] More precisely, an appointment as Secretarial Court Gentleman.

[5] That is, a horse (or, according to some editions, a camel) that can run a thousand Chinese miles in a single day (the Chinese mile is roughly one third of an English mile).

Her army buddies were all flabbergasted:
    "We marched together for these twelve long years
And absolutely had no clue that Mulan was a girl!"

"The male hare wildly kicks its feet;
The female hare has shifty eyes,
But when a pair of hares runs side by side,
Who can distinguish whether I in fact am male or female?"

Translated by Wilt L. Idema

WEI YUANFU

"Song of Mulan" [1]

Shuttle in hand, Mulan heaves a sigh;
"Who is it for this time?" I ask,
wanting to know why she sorrows.
Deeply moved, she composes her face.

"My father is listed in the draft's register,
But his strength and energy daily wane.
How could he journey a myriad miles?
He has a son, but the boy is still too young.

"The steppe sands envelop horses' hooves;
Northern storms crack a man's skin.
My father has grown old, and worn by age;
How can he survive service?"

Mulan goes in place of her father,
Feeds his horse and takes his place in the ranks.
She changes away her white silk skirt;
She washes away her powdered, rouged face.
  Riding the horse, she reports to the garrison;
Filled with noble courage, she wields a sword.
Camping at dawn at the foot of snowy mountains,
Resting at dusk on the bank of Qinghai Lake:
  At night she surprises the captives at Mt. Yanzhi,
And she also captures the Tibetans from Khotan. [2]
The victorious commander in chief returns,
And officers and men can go back home.
  When her father and mother see Mulan,

---

[1] Wei Yuanfu's "Song of Mulan" is written in lines of five syllables, with an occasional admixture of lines of seven syllables. Line spaces in the translation reflect a shift of rhyme in the original. The translation is taken from Wei, 1979, pp. 373–5.

[2] Now known by the modern name Hotan or Hetian in pinyin.

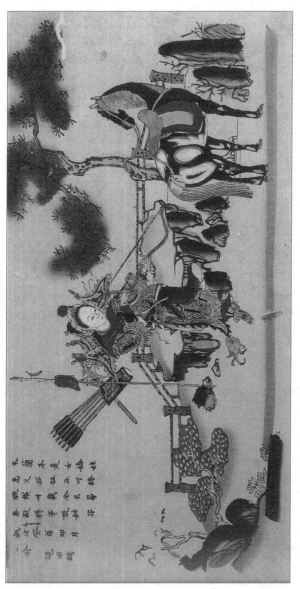

Late Qing New Year print illustration of *Mulan*. The inscription reads:

Mulan was in origin a cute young girl
Who went to the war instead of her father—how admirable!
Fighting far and wide for ten years, she preserved both name and honor.
The peerless general claims to be surnamed "Hua" (flower).

Inscribed by . . . Inkstone Field, on the mao month, guiyou year. Tianjin, Yangliuqing. Late Qing.
Source: Qingmo nianhua huicui (Beijing: Renmin meishu chubanshe, 2000).

Extreme joy turns into sadness and worry.
Mulan can understand the expressions on their faces,
So she discards turban and gauntlet and then tunes the strings:

"Before, I was a hero amongst warriors,
But from now on I'll be your darling girl again!"
Relatives bring wine in congratulations:
"Only now do we know that a daughter is as useful as a son!"

Her old army buddies, assembled outside,
For ten years shared in her trials.
At the outset they swore friendship as brothers,
An oath never broken even in the death of battle!
  But when now on this occasion they see Mulan,
Though the voice is the same, the features are quite different!
Stunned and perplexed, they don't dare approach;
Heaving heavy sighs, in vain filled with wonder.

If in this world the hearts of officials and sons
Could display the same principled virtue as Mulan's,
Their loyalty and filiality would be unbroken;
Their fame would last through the ages—how could it be destroyed?

Translated by Wilt L. Idema

XU WEI

The Female Mulan Joins the Army in Place of Her Father[1]

Act I

Characters:

MULAN, performed by *dan* (young female lead)

XIAOHUAN, performed by *chou* (clown)

HUA HU, performed by *wai* (old male)

MOTHER, performed by *lao* (old female)

YAO'ER, performed by *xiaosheng* (supporting young male)

MUNAN, performed by *tie* (supporting young female)

SOLDIERS

---

[1] *The Female Mulan* is one of the four plays that comprise Xu Wei's *Four Cries of a Gibbon*. The translation is taken from Xu Wei, 1984, pp. 44–59.

Woodblock illustration from a late-Ming edition of Xu Wei's play *The Female Mulan Joins the Army in Place of Her Father* (*Ci Mulan ti fu congjun*). Included in his *Four Cries of a Gibbon* (*Sisheng yuan*).

Source: Guojia tushuguan cang xiqu xiaoshuo banhua xuancui *(Taibei: Guojia tushuguan, 2000).*

(Dan *playing the girl Mulan enters*)

MULAN: My surname is Hua, my name Mulan. Generations ago, in the time of the Western Han, my ancestors, being among those descended from good families of the Six Prefectures,[2] settled here in Hebei's Wei Prefecture.[3] My father's name is Hu, and he is also called Sangzhi. All his life he has loved martial arts and was skilled in literature, and he was at one time a famous "commander of a thousand." He married my mother, from the Jia family, and she gave birth to me.[4] This year, I am barely seventeen years old. Neither my little sister, Munan, or my little brother, Yao'er, have reached adulthood. Yesterday I heard that Black Mountain's head bandit, Leopard Skin, led hundreds of thousands of men on horseback in rebellion and is now calling himself king. Our great Wei's Tuoba khan[5] is calling up troops from our district. The army rolls have been arriving, twelve in a row, scroll after scroll bearing my father's name. As I think of it, my father is not only old, but has no one in the next generation who can carry on for him. When I was young, I was a strong one, and had a bit of smarts, so I followed my father in studying books and martial arts. Now this is my opportunity to repay him. Just take a look at what it says in the books about Qin Xiu[6] and Tiying;[7] one of them willing to die, the other one willing to go to

---

[2] Meaning Longxi 隴西, Tianshui 天水, Anding 安定, Beidi 北地, Shangjun 上郡, and Xihe 西河, in present-day Gansu and Inner Mongolia.

[3] The Wei district was founded in 195 B.C.E. by Han Gaozu, in the Ye jurisdiction. Modern-day Hebei, southwest of Linzhang.

[4] That is to say, Mulan is the daughter of her father's first wife, not of a concubine.

[5] The version from the *Historical Romance of the Sui and Tang* places this story in the Tang dynasty, but Xu Wei places it in a non-Han setting, during the Northern Wei period. The rulers during this period were from the Tuoba family, which was ethnically part of the non-Han nomadic Xianbei tribe federation. They used their word "khan" for emperor, and Mulan is here referring to the emperor when she references the Tuoba khan.

[6] According to a *yuefu* written by Zuo Yannian during the Three Kingdoms period (220–280 C.E.) in Wei, found in the "Miscellaneous Songs" ("Za qu ge ci") section, and titled "Song of the Qin girl, Xiu," Qin Xiu is a girl who avenges the death of her father by killing his murderers in the marketplace. She is incarcerated and given the death penalty, although she is later pardoned.

[7] Tiying is the youngest daughter of the physician Chunyun Yi of the Western Han. Her father was sentenced to mutilation for embezzling government funds and was sent to the capital for execution. Tiying submitted a memorial to Han Wendi (Emperor Wen of the

court to be a slave, both for their fathers' sake. But, weren't those two putting their buns in hairnets? Did they put put on male caps? Didn't they just wear skirts and jackets? There's just one thing: if I were to stand for him, I must have a new bow, horse, spear, sword, gown, and boots—all prepared from scratch. And I'd better go over my martial arts once or twice. Only then can I tell my family about my aims to take dad's place. They will know that there is no alternative and certainly should not take pains to keep me. Where is Xiaohuan?

(Chou *playing a servant, Xiaohuan, enters*)

Xiaohuan! Don't let Father and Mother find out: we are going shopping!

(*Mulan turns offstage and mimes buying things*)
(*Comes back leading Xiaohuan, carrying her packages*)

XIAOHUAN: Miss, where should I tie up the horse?

MULAN: Stable it at Wang San's home, across the way!

[Dianjiangchun][8]

The Xiu girl braved death,
Tiying faced judgment,
        They were both my female companions, in skirts and hairpins.
Standing on the ground, holding up heaven:
What's this about men being heroes?

[Hunjianglong]

The army scrolls are in a dozen,
Roll upon roll, scroll upon scroll, listing my father's name.
He is already aged,
And is plagued by debilitating illness.
To think, how in earlier times,
        He fit an arrow, to hunt the hawk, piercing it with its white-feathered
        shaft.

Han), begging to be her father's substitute to pay off his debt as a slave at court. Wendi was moved, and he thereupon abolished corporal punishment, which was a significant reform of existing Han law.

[8] The arias in Chinese opera are set to existing song tunes. The titles in brackets refer to the melodies in a repertory of aria tunes.

Now, ah,
He leans on a staff, to count the wild geese, counting them against the blue
    sky.
He calls in the chickens, and feeds the dog,
He stays in the village, and minds the fields.
For training falcons, his wrist is too weak,
For chasing hares, his back is too bent.
He leads us sisters by the hand,
He combs the hair of us little girls.
Seeing us in front of mirrors touching up rouge, he laughs out loud,
Hearing about swords raised in battle, his brow furrows, in frowns.
With a long sigh, he says:
"For us parents, North Mang Hill[9] is rearing,
For our girls, the "Bared Belly of the East" has yet to come."[10]

If I want to practice martial arts, I've got to first let out these feet[11] and change
to this pair of boots. Only then will I manage!

(*As she changes footwear, she acts out pain*)

[Youhulu]

Just-removed, the half-folded Tiny Ripple Socks bindings,[12]
How it hurts!
It took me several years to bind together these "Phoenix-head sharps."[13]
Now I quickly turn them into floating boats.[14]
How will I now fill up these boots?

---

[9] This hill north of Luoyang in Henan province is the burial site of royals from the Eastern Han and the Wei and thus functions as a metaphor for death.

[10] The famous calligrapher of the Eastern Jin dynasty (217–420), Wang Xizhi (303–361)
is the source of this allusion. When the emperor's adviser Xi Jian approached Wang's father
about finding a son-in-law for his daughter, Wang told him to go to the Eastern Room to
take a look at his sons. Xi returned to report to the emperor that all of the men were fine,
but they almost all seemed nervous, whereas one of them lay on a couch with his belly ex-
posed. The emperor selected the relaxed one.

[11] This refers to bound feet—an anachronism, as discussed in the Introduction.

[12] A metaphor for bound feet.

[13] Another metaphor for bound feet.

[14] That is, they've become big and flat.

When I return, I'll still want to get married. So what can I do? Well, no need to mope about that! My family has a method for shrinking golden lotuses:[15] just take a bit of saltpeter, boil it, and use it to wash the feet. In this way, we make them even smaller!

(*Sings:*)

Take the raw saltpeter, boil it so it is white like snowflakes,
And in a thrice, you've shrunk them back into golden lotus petals.
In these boots, I'm pretty much steady. Now I'll put on these clothes!

(*Changes clothes, puts on man's felt military cap*)

[Tianxiale]

Dressed up, I daresay I *am* a senior campaigning officer,
Among their ranks, it will be easy to hide.
Hook the belt tightly—
I shall hang my sword on the plates.
The chain mail is pliant and supple,
Its quilted lining is comfy and warm.
I'll bring this armor back, and it will be good enough for my brother to wear.

Clothes and boots are all changed. I've got to practice some swordplay for a bit.

(*Performs swordplay*)

[Nezhaling]

This sword!
How long it's been since I've drawn it,
I've got to say, I thought it wouldn't be easy.
Hoisting it up and giving it a whirl—
Well, it's just like old times.
Why aren't my hands sore with pain,
Used as they are to threading the loom's shuttle?
The girl of Yue still needed the instruction of the white ape.[16]
If I take dad's place in the army, how can I not grasp this green serpent[17]

---

[15] Another metaphor for bound feet.

[16] A legendary heroine, the girl of Yue is a peasant girl who was taught swordplay by a white ape that came to her from the mountains.

[17] That is, the sword.

So fast that round my red skirt I hold this blast of frost![18]

Now I am finished performing with the sword, I had better practice the lance.

(*Acts practicing with lance*)

[Queta zhi]

Whetted until fresh as a leaf of green,
Fixed onto this fine wood staff,
It is as good as any number of rounds of Pear Petals Dancing in Moonlight
And Ten-foot Snake Creeping.[19]
Wait, wait, until my feet have unfolded,
And with big steps I can stride again,
And then with one turn of my body, I will push over the tip of Black Mountain.

Ah, arrows! I can't practice them here. I'll just have to try to pull the bowstring.
I will see how my way with the bow and string compares to the old days.

(*Acts pulling bow*)

[Jishengcao]

The thumb ring is thin,
The frame's ends are rounded.
With one fist closed tight, I grab the "Yellow Snake."[20]
For a single arrow, a full eagle's tail has been pulled out.[21]
One outstretched arm holds forth with the strength of the white ape.
Singing drawn-out songs, the hero enters the pass,
Then, only then, will I reveal my Tianshan arrows.[22]

---

[18] Her swordplay will be so swift that the glints around her will blend into a whirl of frost-like silver, set off by her red skirt.

[19] Various fighting methods involving lances.

[20] The character translated as "cast," *cuan*, is the same character used for casting a shuttle (as in weaving), but here it is used to refer to the snakeskin-covered bow.

[21] Arrows were traditionally made with eagle tail feathers as fletchings.

[22] During Tang Taizong's reign, one of his generals, Xue Rengui, was surrounded on Tian Mountain (Tianshan) under attack by the Tiele. He was challenged to fight ten members of the Tiele cavalry. The three arrows he shot killed the three top generals, and this show of skill caused the rest of the Tiele to surrender.

As for riding a donkey or a horse, it is familiar enough to me. Even so, I've got to get the posture of jumping astride the saddle.

(*Mounts horse in the posture of sitting astride a horse*)

[Yao]

Embroidered front and back, my horse-riding vest,
Inlaid with coral, my horse-urging whip,
This costume is not army issue.
So with these two leather reins I'll control my unicorn tightly,
And through millions of mountains I'll catch alive a monkey companion.[23]
With this one bit and bridle, I'll trample out the foxes from their den.
I will only reveal that a lovely girl was the one in the saddle when I
    return home.[24]
Who, then, will not call me a great hero?

Everything is taken care of now. I have to call Father and Mother to come out so I can talk to them.

(*Addressing backstage, she asks father, mother, younger brother, and younger sister to come out*)
(*Wai playing father,* lao *playing mother,* xiaosheng *playing brother, and* tie *playing the younger sister enter. Upon seeing her, they are surprised.*)

MOTHER: Child! Why are you dressed up like this today? You have unbound your feet! How strange! How strange!

MULAN: Mother! Father is supposed to join the army: how can he not go?

MOTHER: He is old already, how *can* he go?

MULAN: Could little sister or little brother be made to go?

MOTHER: You're mad! How are two as young as they are able to go?

MULAN: Things being that way, then no one will go.

---

[23] It was thought that exhausted horses, if allowed to sleep for too long, would become severely ill; therefore, the horse's keeper would house a monkey in the stables with the horse to distract it and keep it awake, making a monkey part of riding paraphernalia.

[24] It is impossible to replicate in English the play on words and sounds here. The word for "beautiful," which is definitely a feminine adjective (*jiao* 嬌) sounds similar (indicated by the shared sound element) to the word meaning saddle (*jiao* 驕).

MOTHER: That's precisely why we are at our wits' end. Your father is ready to hang himself from worry!

MULAN: The way I am now . . . can I go?

MOTHER: Child! I know well your abilities. You could indeed go. (*Crying*) It's just that . . . how can two old folks like us bear to let you go? And another thing, if you go . . . you're still a girl. Through a thousand provinces and a million miles, you'll be marching with men and keeping their constant company—breakfasting together in the morning, lodging together at night—you cannot prevent your you-know-what from showing! Don't you think that this will create problems?

MULAN: Mom! Don't worry. I will return to you still a virgin.

(*They weep together*)
(*Two soldiers enter*)

SOLDIER: Is this the Hua residence?

FATHER: Why do you ask?

SOLDIER: We are also recruits. Our home office said that in this ward there is a Hua Hu and told us to come and hasten him so that we may all travel together, so hurry up.

MULAN: Brothers, sit a while! Allow me to prepare a few things, and I'll be ready to go. Xiaohuan, go fetch my horse!

(*Mulan readies her military equipment*)
(*Everyone watches*)

PARENTS: Fine horse! Fine arms! You'll certainly be a success, returning to hurrahs. No matter what, you must regularly write to us, and spare us both from worrying. Now, we'd like to drink a toast to you, but things are so helter-skelter. I've sent Xiaohuan to go buy you some hot buns. Bring them with you for munching on the road. I'll put these needles and thread in your bag, and you'll be prepared if you get a rip in your clothes, or a break in your armor!

TWO SOLDIERS: Hurry up!

(*Family members weep in parting, then leave first*)
(*Mulan goes to meet the soldiers*)

MULAN: Elder brothers, thanks for waiting such a long while! Let's mount our horses and be off.

(*Mulan gets on the horse and starts on her way*)
(*The soldiers secretly confer*)

SOLDIERS: This Hua Hu doesn't look bad at all. He doesn't look like a senior officer, but he'd be a nice morsel. Tomorrow we can take him to meet our needs.

MULAN:

[Yao]

I'm no further from home than a shot from an arrow,
But I hear the sputtering Yellow River's flow.
The horse lowers his head, and I point far off to where the goose drops into the reeds.
My iron armor is unlined—suddenly there appears a fleck of frosty crystal.
From the intensity of the sorrows of parting, my peach-flower face has become drawn.
If I for a moment think of these tightly stitched clothes,[25]
Two rows of tears drip from their pearl strings.

[Liu yao xu]

Ai! The smell of face powder still lingers on my face;
I try to wash off the mark left by my hair ornament.
It still isn't gone even after a whole day.
But I have been twisted into a veritable man, and in great haste, I mount
    my horse, astride the saddle.
In my boots are planted a golden whip,
My feet push against the bronze rings,
Dropping the needle's point,
I've slung on my strung bow.[26]

---

[25] An allusion to Meng Jiao's (751–814) "Song for the Traveler":
    The thread in his mother's hand,
    Sews clothes for the traveler.
    Close together, these tight stitches,
    fearing a late return.
    Who can say that the inch-long heart of grass
    requites three months of spring's rays?
This poem is the classic exposition on a mother's love.

[26] Replacing one kind of "needle" and "thread" with another.

Before I meet anyone, I am prepared to meet him by bending my back;
I cannot use anymore the curtsying I did in my woman's skirts.
I don't fear the mandarin ducks becoming a pair and asking for marriage,
I'm more concerned about the burning need to pee and poop.[27]
I need a ruse.

[Yao]

Brothers! While we've been talking,
And without urging the whip,
We've crossed ten thousand green mountains like dots, and
Neared "Five Zhang"[28] Red Pass.
Where the sunlight rests on the city wall's parapets,
Several banner flags are raised.
In tattered caps, and worn shirts,
They are not very intimidating,
This must be an officer of the guard!
Is he not like us, one of the same kind?
Relying on our youth,
Relying on Blue Heaven,
Not fearing hardship,
Not loving money,
Yet we all head toward recognition, for which our portraits will hang up in
    Lingyan Tower.[29]
Isn't this better than scheming and robbing someone of his command, and
    stealing someone's glory?
It is worth much more than wealth and position, which is after all
    decreed by Heaven.
Even if the Black Mountain Bandits' crimes are broad as heaven,
They began as nothing more than mere thoughts in the mind.

(*Acts out asking*)

---

[27] Thus revealing her female genitalia to the soldiers.

[28] A "zhang" is a Chinese measurement equivalent to 11 feet 9 inches.

[29] This refers to portraits commissioned by Tang Taizong of twenty-four meritorious officials. Here, Mulan says that she and the other soldiers are not looking for glory, but only to serve their ruler.

[Yao]

Where are we now?
Feet and inches away, but
Seeming halfway to heaven,
The long slope ahead winds like a coiled snake.
It must be that the commander in chief is seated atop the platform,
A little Tiying is about to meet a great commanding officer.
By now my heart is shaken,
In time I will get comfortable with a warrior's heart.
Commanding a thousand men and horses,
I will sweep across Black Mountain in battle,
I shall sweep away the traces of old rouge from my flower cheeks with my
    sable cap.

ALL: While we were talking, we happily arrived at the commander's camp. We
shall first select a place to set up, and tomorrow we shall all go together to see
our commander. (*Exeunt*)

Act II

Characters:

XIN PING, performed by *wai*

MULAN, performed by *dan*

LEOPARD SKIN, performed by *jing* (male "painted face")

EUNUCH, performed by *chou*

MOTHER, performed by *lao*

YAO'ER, performed by *xiaosheng*

MUNAN, performed by *tie*

WANG LANG, performed by *sheng* (young male lead)

XIAOHUAN, performed by *chou*

SOLDIERS

(Wai *playing the commanding general enters*)

XIN PING: I am the "Subduing the East" commanding general, Xin Ping. Our ruler ordered me to lead 100,000 brave troops to kill the Black Mountain bandits, and I have been victorious in every battle. But we can't do anything about the chief bandit, Leopard Skin, who has hidden himself behind high, steep cliffs and won't come out from behind their walls. The other day, three thousand braves newly arrived, and I will appoint them after trying out their martial skills. There is a Hua Hu, who seemed capable. Now I am about to roll out this catapult, to fire on those steep cliffs above. This chief bandit will have no choice but to come out and fight. When the troops are drawn up against each other in battle formation, I will have Hua Hu cut through in the middle on horseback, and we are bound to capture Leopard Skin at the first roll of the drum. Where are Hua Hu and the new soldiers?

(Mulan *and the group of soldiers enter and kneel*)

XIN PING: Hua Hu! Tomorrow I will attack Black Mountain. After two rounds of battle, you have to let your horse gallop and dash into the troops.

22

You will be sure to capture the bandit chief alive. Then I will recommend you to the emperor, and your reward will not be meager. If you disobey, you will be beheaded.

MULAN: Yes, sir. I have received your command!

XIN PING: Then let's raise the troops and go forth!

[Qingjiang yin]

Black Mountain's little bandit is truly shortsighted!
He continues to hide himself—what can he accomplish?
When the flower opens, butterflies fill the branches.
When the tree falls, the monkeys scatter off.
The more you hide, the more I'll seek the sight of you.

CHORUS OF SOLDIERS:

[To the same tune]

Black Mountain's little bandit is truly farsighted!
Left or right, he's used to getting defeated.
All day long he feels no shame at all,
And in all three meals, gobbles his fill.
The more you seek him out, the more he hides and watches what will
    happen.

Your Lordship! We have arrived at the bandit hideout.

XIN PING: Tell the troops to raise the catapult and fire!

(*They fire the catapult. A* jing *playing the bandit chief thrice comes out in front of the ranks to fight. Mulan dashes out in front and captures him.*)

XIN PING: Call back the troops to return!

CHORUS OF SOLDIERS:

[To the same tune]

Our great leader is truly farsighted,
Only after careful calculation did he act.
This bandit was a false case of: When the flower opens, butterflies fill the
    branches,
In truth, he was like: When the tree falls, the monkeys scatter off.
Returning with a victory song, we share in his pride.

XIN PING:

[To the same tune]

My gathered soldiers, the great sight that you witnessed a moment ago
Means we'll have an extra string of cash every month.
No more "all day long he knows no shame";
I'll make sure each man shall have three meals to gobble his fill.
When it comes to weighing merits, it is Hua Hu who claims the greatest
    share of credit.

(*Arriving at the capital, sound of bells and drums. They act out an audience at court.*)

XIN PING: (*memorializing to the throne*) The humble "Subduing the East" commanding general, Xin Ping, respectfully reports: by Your Majesty's grace, we were
sent to march against the bandits from Black Mountain and have fully pacified
them. The bandit chief, Leopard Skin, was indeed captured by my soldier, Hua
Hu, in front of the ranks; he has been brought here for your disposal. As for
the other worthy men, I have put down their names on the registers and made
distinctions according to their merits, and hope you will make your decisions
accordingly.

(Chou *playing eunuch presents emperor's edict*)

EUNUCH: His Majesty commands: you have gained great merit in eradicating the bandits, and We have specially enfeoffed[30] you as the marquis of Chang-
shan. We present you with a tablet of office for perpetual inheritance. Hua Hu
shall be the secretarial court officer in the Imperial Secretariat. Bearing in mind
his many years of laboring in military service, We order that he return home
posthaste to rest for three months, then await the new appointment. He will be
given official cap and girdle, and, following this, he and Xin Ping may give thanks
for Our imperial grace. Leopard Skin will be beheaded. As for the other wor-
thies, We will act once their cases are verified.

(*Mulan puts on official cap and girdle*)
(*General and Mulan give thanks, and receive the decree.* Chou *exits.*)

MULAN: I, Hua Hu, am grateful to Your Honor for raising me up with this
recommendation to receive imperial glory and grace beyond my due. But as I am

---

[30] Given a title and stipend.

anxious about visiting my parents, I cannot go to your office to give thanks. Allow me first to kowtow to you here, and allow me to one day repay you as a dog or horse would its master.

XIN PING: What you achieved you did on your own. What does it have to do with me? Because we are in such haste, I, too, cannot send you gifts to congratulate you properly.

MULAN: Today you have helped me greatly.

XIN PING: I have done no more than lend wind to the sail of a boat going with the current.

(*Xin Ping exits first*)

MULAN:

[**To the same tune**]

Everything is—when I think of it—an illusion, after all;
Why should I boast that I succeeded in this scheme?
The "I" who killed bandits, and captured their king,
Was a woman who changed place with a man.
After all, these successes did not cost me a drop of sweat.

(*Two soldiers hurry onstage*)

SOLDIERS: Sir Hua! How well you have done!

MULAN: Why are you two so late in coming?

SOLDIERS: We two awaited successful investigations, and now we have acquired centurion positions. We hope that you will look out for us!

MULAN: Happy news! Now we can travel together.

SOLDIERS:

[**To the same tune**]

When you think of it, Big Brother Hua is really weird!
Whether he's pissing or shitting, he won't allow anyone to watch.
(*Companions to each other*) That's a mark of gentility for you!
If heaven gives birth to a worthy man,
It brings luck to his three companions.

The two of us, with offices puny as sesame seeds, raised our eyes to take a look at him.

MULAN:

[To the same tune]

How am I, Hua Hu, so weird?
I only know of one thing that is weird.
Right next to my home, in a temple,
There is a protecting demon statue, whose face
Suddenly changed into Chang'e's![31]

SOLDIERS: Truly?

MULAN: If you don't believe me, when we reach my home I will bring you to see it.

(*Exit*)
(*Father, mother, Xiaohuan enter*)

PARENTS: Since the time our girl, Mulan, left, there hasn't been a bit of news. The good thing is that at New Year's, Minister Wang's son, Mr. Wang, impressed that Mulan was so filial as to take her father's place, sought to be affianced with her. Who would have thought that Mr. Wang would go on to succeed in the "Wise and Good" and "Literary Scholarship" categories?[32] Now he is home, visiting his parents with the title "collator of the Imperial Library." Mulan, too, has been gone for more than ten years. With the two of them each grown into man and woman, and of marrying age, this is no light matter! But how do we get her to come home, so that we can conclude this betrothal and die with a clear conscience?

(*Two soldiers enter with Mulan*)

SOLDIERS: Sir Hua! We've arrived at your home! We two will take our leave and go!

MULAN: What kind of talk is this? Please have a seat in the left chamber, and wait until noon to go on.

---

[31] From a masculine protective demon (*jingang*) statue to that of the feminine goddess of the moon, Chang'e.

[32] These exam categories can be understood roughly as "Civics" and "Composition."

(*Soldiers assent, stepping aside so as to indicate leaving room*)
(*Mulan advances and sees parents*)

MOTHER: (*to maid*) Girl! Quick, call Second Sister and Third Brother to come out, tell them that Big Sister has come back!

(*Maid calls younger sister and brother, who enter*)
(*Mulan, facing her mirror, changes back to female makeup, then bows in greeting to her parents*)

MULAN:

[Shua haier]

Your child left, cutting down bandits with martial sword,
Wiping them away like the wind scattering clouds;
I captured the bandit chief alive, then left the capital:
This black gauze cap came from the khan himself.

MOTHER: Your office, what office is it?

MULAN:
It is Secretarial Gentleman. Mother!
I have been bound up tightly so many years in a hall with the nightly rain of
     pear-blossom petals,
But I return to you as before, a little box of dogwood bud in spring winds.[33]
How could I shame my parents?

MOTHER: My child, to think of what you have done!

MULAN:
I don't mean to boast that . . . true gold withstands fire,
Or that it well compares to . . . the red lotus emerging from the mud.[34]

(*Bows in greeting to brother and sister*)

[Er sha]

When I left, you were just a little thing,
Now I've returned, your shoulders reach mine,
Right now you are quite ready to go to battle on Father's behalf.

---

[33] That is, still a virgin after all these years.

[34] The lotus is prized because it blooms pure and unblemished in spite of the mud from which it springs.

Sister, thank you for supporting our two elderly parents,
Brother, all of our generation should consider you its number one.
When I left the city, I could not find time to buy some perfume or
    handkerchiefs.
To give to sister: just a package of face powder,
And for brother: two boxes of pine-soot ink.

(*The two soldiers hurry onstage*)

SOLDIERS: Sir Hua! You were a girl all along! We lived with you for a dozen years, and none of us knew at all. So it turns out the demon that you spoke of on the road, who turned into Chang'e, was this riddle! You are the greatest miracle of all time. It will be known the world over, and everyone will remember you.

MULAN:

[San sha]

It is said that between men and women, even their mats shouldn't touch,
But when there's no other option, one must use expedient means.
The clever blossom hid securely from the butterflies' ardor.
In Father's place, I, ah! Was like the younger brother-in-law for whom
It's impossible to let go of his sister-in-law's hand, to save her from
    drowning.[35]
Toward you men, ah! You were like fire raging for dry tinder—how could I
    not deceive you?
    I was like the heron which is seen only when it soars from the snow.[36]
In total we were together for ten years,
That makes for half a marriage.

SOLDIERS: With them so busy, we should make ourselves scarce. So we won't take our leave, but just go!

(*Exit*)

---

[35] Mencius' clarification that whereas men and women should keep a distance between them, extenuating circumstances (such as the woman's risk of drowning!) could cause a man to extend his hand to touch his sister-in-law.

[36] This line appears in Xu Wei's play *The Mad Drummer Plays the Yuyang Triple Roll* (*Mi Heng*) as well.

XIAOHUAN: Mr. Wang has come to offer congratulations.

MOTHER: This is the son-in-law that I wrote to you about the other day. I was about to invite him over, so that you could have your wedding. What perfect timing!

(*A* sheng *in official cap and girdle playing Mr. Wang enters and sees them*)

MOTHER: Mr. Wang ... stay your greetings! I have just looked at the almanac for an auspicious day. You two are as old as cast bronze elephants,[37] so let's make ourselves a family today! Quick, quick, bow and greet each other!

(*Mulan turns her back, shyly*)

MOTHER: Child! After a dozen years as an officer, what do you have to be shy about?

(*Mulan turns and bows*)

MULAN:

[Si sha]

Barely reunited with my family,
Who would have dreamed it would be a wedding?
Now, meeting this way, how can I help but perspire with embarrassment?
I've long known of your honors in literature at court,
I'm ashamed that I've returned from the din of battle.
I cannot match up with this Eastern Couch[38] mate.
I shall serve you as the Divine Immortal flutist,[39]
Don't fear that I'll be a little sister like Sun Quan's.[40]

---

[37] A Ming turn of phrase indicating that they are of age.

[38] Another reference to Wang Xizhi (see note 10), the ideal son-in-law.

[39] Xiao Shi (the Divine Immortal) is a legendary figure skilled in *xiao* flute playing, who could imitate a phoenix cry on the flute. Nongyu, the daughter of Duke Mu of Qin, was also a skilled *xiao* player, and the duke gave his daughter in marriage to Xiao Shi. One morning, Nongyu mounted a phoenix and Xiao Shi mounted a dragon, and they flew off together.

[40] During the Three Kingdoms period, the Wu kingdom ruler, Sun Quan, had a younger sister who was skilled in martial arts. She was given by Sun Quan to Liu Bei in marriage. On their wedding night, Liu Bei found their bridal chamber filled with weapons, which Liu Bei asked her to remove. In spite of these beginnings, the two had a loving marriage.

[Wei]

I was a woman till I was seventeen,
Was a man for twelve more years.
Passed under thousands of glances,
Which of them could tell cock from hen?
Only now do I believe that a distinction between male and female isn't told by
  the eyes.
Who was it really occupied Black Mountain Top?
The girl Mulan went to war for her pop.
The affairs of the world are all such a mess,
Muddling boy and girl is what this play does best.[41]

Translated by Shiamin Kwa

---

[41] The play is followed in the earliest printed edition by the following additional notes: "When Mulan tries out a weapon and changes clothes and shoes, she absolutely must do wonderful kicks and jumps. When each part of the stage work is done, then she will sing, otherwise it will be a mess."

ANONYMOUS

Mu Lan Joins the Army (1903)[1]

Part I

Drafting Troops

Mocking Elder Brother

Taking Leave of One's Parents

Setting Out for the Border

Characters:

ZHAO JING, performed by supporting *jing*

MU LAN'S FATHER, performed by old *sheng*

MU LAN'S MOTHER, performed by old *dan*

MU LAN, performed by *dan*

MU LAN'S YOUNGER SISTER, performed by additional *dan*

MU SHU, performed by little *chou*

---

[1] The translation is based on A Ying, 1959, pp. 294–303.

(*Zhao Jing enters in military dress, whipping his horse and holding a flag of command*)

ZHAO JING:

(*Prelude couplet*)

Executing the orders of the imperial court;
Drafting troops throughout the wide world.

(*Speaks:*) I am Zhao Jing, an officer under the command of General Huo, the great marshal before the throne of the Son of Heaven of the Great Han. At the order of the imperial court I am widely drafting men for the army. On my mission I have used the pretext of requiring one adult male from every household. These common people, who all fear death, beseech me to do them a favor, so I have received quite some bribes. I have now arrived in Dingtao County. In this county, I've learned, lives a rich man of modest means, who has achieved his wealth by diligence and thrift. He has only one daughter, who is called Mu Lan. She is bewitchingly beautiful, and she has no brother who can join the army for its northern campaign. I'll have to use once again the pretext of requiring one adult male from every household and extract a few more bribes. (*Acts out nodding his head and smiling to himself*) Let me apply the whip to this horse, and I'll be off! (*Acts out whipping his horse and circling the stage*) (*Exits*)

(*Mu Lan's father and Mu Lan's mother enter with Mu Lan, in simple costume, and Mu Lan's younger sister, with hanging bangs and gaudily dressed*)
(*Prelude couplet*)

MU LAN'S FATHER: Into old age I've been a commoner in the countryside.

MU LAN'S MOTHER: The whole family happily manifests Heaven's norms.

(*Mu Lan's father and Mu Lan's mother act out sitting down together*) (*Mu Lan and Mu Lan's younger sister act out paying their respects*)

MU LAN'S MOTHER: Sit down by our side! (*Mu Lan and Mu Lan's younger sister act out sitting down*)

MU LAN'S FATHER: My children, your cousin Boshi has not come home these last few days, and I have no idea where he may be hanging out. These last few days my eyes, I felt, were seeing better, but my heart is truly filled with worries. Just think, my strength is diminishing day by day, and my energy is less and less with every day. If something untoward should happen to me, I have no idea what kind of suffering might be the fate of you two girls.

MU LAN: Daddy, don't worry! Cousin Boshi may be idly loafing about now that he is still young, but I believe he is a real man full of enthusiasm and fervor. As long as you, dear Father, don't forget that he is our closest relative and instruct him in a stern, fatherly way, he is bound to turn out all right in the future!

MU LAN'S FATHER: My child, you are mistaken! (*Sings:*)

A true man is characterized by his noble courage:
What he says while seated he'll execute in action.
Since ancient times trouble comes from empty talk;
Without serious study nobody later turns out right.

MU LAN: Dear Father! (*Sings:*)

The nature of a young man is not yet established:
Once he drops the butcher's knife, he's a Buddha.
If you teach and instruct him in a fatherly way,
All of a sudden the blunt iron will turn into gold!

(*Mu Shu enters in military garb*)
(*Prelude couplet*)

I'm sneaking away from places of song and dance;
Washing my eyes by banks of streams and clouds.

(*Speaks:*) I am Mu Shu, and my style is Boshi.[2] As a child I lost both my parents, and growing up I have loved the martial arts. With my roaming knight-errant friends we form bands and gangs, and when discussing the situation of the world, we blame Heaven and Earth. I have been raised by my uncle, but today I have almost turned twenty. It's too bad that my uncle is such a tightfisted old scrooge. He doesn't have any son of his own, but he is unwilling to let me freely spend his money—I have no idea why this old guy without a son is holding on to his money! This morning I heard people in the marketplace tell that the empire is drafting soldiers to go on a northern campaign and fight the bandits. But

---

[2] Upper-class men in traditional China would have at least two names. They received their personal name (*ming*) soon after birth; this name they would often use for self-designation. Upon reaching adulthood, they would choose their adult name or style (*zi*), which would be used by others when addressing them. Mentioning both personal name and style is a common element in self-introductions.

I eat my own rice,[3] so why should I make any effort on behalf of the state? I'd better sneak away and hide myself for a while at home and then later make new plans. While talking I have already arrived at the gate of our house. (*Acts out entering the gate*) (*Acts out greeting*) (*Speaks:*) Uncle and Aunt, please accept my best wishes.

MU LAN'S FATHER and MU LAN'S MOTHER: Dear son, you've come home!

MU LAN: (*rises, and speaks:*) Cousin Boshi, you have come home! That's great, because my parents were concerned about you. (*Acts out greeting*)

MU LAN'S FATHER: My son Boshi! (*Sings:*)

Ever since you left home, we never received any news,
And as a result, we were constantly thinking about you.
We were afraid you might suffer from hunger and cold—
White-haired and waiting, we were filled with anxiety!
  From now on you should tame your unbridled mind,
And make sure to glorify your parents by making a name.
A man's achievement all depends on his personal efforts;
If you don't put in the effort, how can you achieve fame?

MU LAN: Cousin! (*Sings:*)

My dear elder brother, now please attentively listen to me.
You have to take your closest relatives into consideration!
Alas, our father and mother are now in a desperate situation,
And they have no other son whom they can call their own.
  All-under-heaven is in turmoil, and no region is pacified—
You should make every effort to make your plans quickly.
You're a man in the strength of his years, filled with vigor:
If you do not grab this opportunity, you will never succeed.

(*The military officer Zhao Jing, carrying the flag of command, enters*)

ZHAO JING: Here I have arrived outside the gate of Mu Lan. Let me give them a scare! (*Roars like the Gorges:*) Anybody inside?

(*Mu Lan's father and Mu Lan's mother act out being frightened*) (*Mu Shu acts out being so scared that he falls to the ground*)

---

[3] In other words, I have never received an appointment or a salary from the state, so there is no obligation for me to repay any favor shown to me by the state.

(*Mu Lan and Mu Lan's younger sister act out being flustered; they speak to Mu Shu and Mu Lan's father*)

MU LAN: Daddy, there is someone at the door calling for you.

(*Mu Lan's father acts out holding his staff with shaking hands and greeting the officer, but being unable to speak*) (*Zhao Jing enters, and Mu Lan and Mu Lan's younger sister act out avoiding him [by leaving]*)

ZHAO JING: At the order of His Majesty the Emperor I have come to your district to draft adult males. If you have any son or cousin who will join the army, quickly report his name!

MU LAN'S FATHER: (*replying in a quaking voice:*) Yes, yes! I have one full nephew named Mu Shu.

MU SHU: (*on the ground replying in a panic:*) I'm not, not, not his nephew, I won't go!

ZHAO JING: Tell him to report for duty at our garrison tomorrow in the third quarter of the hour of noon. If he tries to flee or to hide himself, this will mean you will have transgressed military law, and I will have you, old fart, arrested and beheaded!

MU LAN'S FATHER: (*replying in a quaking voice:*) Yes, yes!

ZHAO JING: (*leaving the house and acting out being surprised*) I had clearly been informed that Mu Lan had no elder brother, so where did she find this cousin? Let's wait till tomorrow at the barracks and question him once again. (*Exits*)

(*Mu Lan's father acts out wiping away his tears. Mu Lan's mother, Mu Lan, and Mu Lan's younger sister act out appearing again and act out helping Mu Shu to his feet.*)

MU LAN'S FATHER: Dear Boshi! (*Sings:*)

He calls out: My dear Boshi, you now listen to my order!
This is your opportunity to go out and to have a career.
If you now go out and exterminate all those barbarians,
You'll be ennobled as a marquis with a hundred towns!

(*Speaks:*) My son, this is your lucky moment! Quickly get ready for your departure, and don't miss out on this chance to establish merit. My only wish is that you will leave early and return soon, so we, these old people, may witness your glory! (*Sings:*)

Dear Boshi, quickly set out on your many-day journey!
Throughout your life you've said you have the abilities.
Right now it's the moment to display your statesmanship,
And I want you to go out and make a determined effort,
So history books for all eternity will transmit your fame.

MU SHU: Dear Uncle! (*Sings:*)

He addressed him as dear uncle, please let me explain,
I am only a little student of books, so young of years!
You can't believe the empty words of my earlier days—
Why do you want me to be a soldier and join the army?
    In case I would lose my life out there on the battlefield,
You'd be bereft of the only person who can be your heir.

Dear Uncle! (*Acts out weeping*) Dear Uncle,

You, you, you have to come up with some secret scheme,
Because I desperately cling to this miserable life of mine.
Please go and bribe that officer, and ask him for his mercy;
Give him some gold and silver so he will go on his way!

MU LAN'S FATHER: (*acting out turning toward Mu Lan and pointing*) Now what?
I knew all along that he would turn out to be a good-for-nothing. (*Acts out wiping away his tears*)

MU LAN: Cousin Boshi! (*Sings to the rapid beat:*)

Your little sister has something she wants to say to you;
Please listen attentively, and don't be secretly annoyed.
Since ancient times great heroes, Chinese and foreign,
All have been willing to risk their life for their country.
    How come you are such a weakling and good-for-nothing,
Who clings to life afraid of death, making people laugh?
They'll say you're just a big straw bag, big but of no use!
It's too bad that I am still only so very young indeed,
And that on top of that I was born as a beautiful girl.
    If in my current existence I had only been born as a boy,

MU SHU: Then what? (*Mu Lan resumes singing:*)

I would grasp in my hands a lance or a spear,
I would hang at my waist a bow and a sword,

And all alone on a single horse beyond Yangguan,[4]
Kill off those barbarians so none was left to flee!

MU SHU: Little Sister, don't brag. You're a girl, so what do you know about
the sufferings of the battlefield? (*Sings to the rapid beat:*)

Dear little sister, now please don't be upset at me,
Please keep your mouth shut and don't blabber on.
If you'd raise your sword,
    Spur on your horse,
        And arrive at the border,
Your soul, too,
    Immediately would fly off
        To beyond the ninth heaven.
If I indeed am afraid to die and make people laugh,
Why don't you
    In my place
        Join the army and put on armor?

MU LAN: (*singing to the rapid beat:*)

Dear elder brother, there's no need to mock me now:
Since ancient times there have been female generals.
I definitely want to report my name at the garrison,
And with raised sword assist Commander in Chief Huo!

MU LAN'S MOTHER: My child, you are a girl, so how can you go?

MU LAN: I definitely can go. I have always wanted to join the army and shame
those men. (*Acts out kneeling down and taking her leave*)

(*Mu Lan's father and Mu Lan's mother act out weeping*) (*Mu Lan and Mu Shu act out exchanging clothes*)

MU LAN:

In front of the hall I take leave of my father and mother,
And I take leave of my elder brother and younger sister.

---

[4] Yangguan is the name of a border station on the western edge of Gansu. It was immortalized in a popular parting song by Wang Wei (d. 761).

(Acts out taking leave of Mu Shu and Mu Lan's younger sister) (Mu Shu acts out imitating female gait and dress)

MU LAN:

I have something to say that I want to impress on you:
Elder brother and younger sister should live in harmony.
  Elder Brother, from now on you must learn to behave,
Don't go and join your old cronies for all kinds of mischief.
When I go and establish major merit on Rouge Ridge,
It will be you, Elder Brother, who'll enjoy that great fame.
  I will in final analysis remain a woman, so in my thoughts
I will always be at home, filially serving my two parents.
Constantly, morning and evening, make sure they are fine,
And comfort our parents whenever they are depressed.
  If I will be lucky enough to survive and come back home,
I will once again express my feelings over our separation.
At this moment I cannot fully express my heart's feelings,
As I am about to leave for the army to report my name.

(Mu Lan acts out weeping as she leaves, acts out walking, acts out turning around to look, and exits) (Mu Lan's father, Mu Lan's mother, and Mu Lan's younger sister act out waving their hands)

MU SHU: She is gone. What are you still standing here for? *(Pulls Mu Lan's father and Mu Lan's mother away)*

MU LAN'S YOUNGER SISTER: Slowly, Cousin Boshi! Slowly! Listen to what I have to say! *(Sings:)*

When a man lacks all shame he is truly despicable:
You truly are just a silverlike wax-headed spear![5]
Hearing about barbarians, you retract your head,[6]
Unwilling to shed your blood on the battlefield.

Dear brother Boshi,

It's not that I, your little sister, am mocking you,
But from now on I wouldn't go and brag anymore.

---

[5] A "silverlike, wax-headed spear" may look very pretty but is of no use on the battlefield.

[6] That is, you act like a turtle. "Turtle" was a common curse word meaning "pimp" or "cuckold."

You said you were filled with hatred for the enemy,
But I see your courage is less than that of a pig or dog,
It doesn't measure up to that of one single beautiful girl.

(*Acts out mocking Mu Shu by pulling a face at him*)

MU LAN'S FATHER and MULAN'S MOTHER: Little girl, this is just the way he is, so don't mock him. Let's go inside. (*Exeunt*)

Part II

The Lost Battle

The Victory Celebration

The Court Audience

The Glorious Return

Characters:

MU LAN, performed by *dan*

HUO QUBING, performed by (old) *sheng*

ZHAO JING, performed by supporting *jing*

GUARDS, performed by extras

KHAN, performed by *jing*

BARBARIANS, performed by extras

WEI QING, performed by young *sheng*

HAN SOLDIERS, performed by extras

A BARBARIAN SPY, performed by *chou*

EUNUCHS, performed by extras

EMPEROR, performed by *jing*

(*Mu Lan changed into male costume, in military dress, with a bow and arrows on her back, a sword at her side, and carrying a lance*)

MU LAN:

(*Prelude couplet*)

Cheeks like lotus flowers and a waist like a willow:
While a helmet covers my head I brandish a sword.

(*Speaks:*) I am Mu Lan, and I am determined to join the army in place of my father[7] and to establish merit beyond the border by exterminating the caitiffs. Since I have taken leave of my parents, I am on my way to the garrison to report for duty. Who could have thought that I as a girl would have such a great opportunity today!

(*Sings to the slow beat as the* suona[8] *is played backstage:*)

Storm-driven dust
        Extends to the Central Plain,
                An endless expanse of yellow sand;
The breath of death is rising,
        Spreading east, west, north, south,
                To the very edges of the earth.
Who could have foreseen
        That the written order to serve
                Would drop down in front of my embroidery window?
It promptly filled me,
        This female hero,
                With an all-overpowering, towering rage!
At the shortest moment
        I had taken my leave
                Of my white-haired aged parents.
I've abandoned
        My inner-chamber companions,
                Who do embroidery and pick their flowers;

---

[7] Curiously, in Part I the imperial emissary Zhao Jing never claims that Mu Lan's father has to serve!

[8] For a description of the *suona*, see Wichmann, 1991, p. 232.

I've abandoned
    The application of rouge and powder,
        The burned incense and fragrant musk;
I've abandoned
    The singing shirt and dancing sleeves,
        And the lute with its many strings.
I've come to compete in
    Ascending the terrace with raised sword,[9]
        Lifting the lance and grabbing a horse;
I've come to see
    The forest of spears and trees of sabers,
        And people killed in great numbers.
I've come to compete in
    The number of heads of slain fighters,
        For the reputation of being a man;
I've come to hear
    The rustling poplars of the border lands,
        And the barbarian reed pipe of the steppe.
Just look at me
    As I look around, filled with confidence,
        Raising winds and clouds by my roar;
Just look at me
    As I earn merit, achieve noble rank,
        And establish a mansion with rows of banners;
Just look at me
    As I will lead the captured barbarians
        To bow down at the emperor's feet!

(*Speaks:*) On this journey . . . (*Sings:*)

I definitely will
    Slaughter the dragon with my bare hands,
        And achieve merit in this acrobatic performance,
But who will know
    That I am one
        As light as a swallow,
            As beautiful as a flower!

---

[9] In order to emphasize the importance of the occasion, Liu Bang appointed Han Xin as his commander in chief on a raised terrace.

(*Speaks:*) I am so elated! (*Twirls her lance and exits*)

(*Huo Qubing, with a red face and white beard, dressed as commander, enters with guards and the officer Zhao Jing*)

HUO QUBING:

(*Prelude couplet*)

A general in the field, a chancellor at court:
My painted portrait is seen in Unicorn Hall.

(*While music is played backstage, he acts out ascending the commander's seat. Speaks:*)

In the Han camp the great flag and pointed banners are arrayed;
Ennobled to the highest rank I command the walls of the border.
When I as general issue an order, even the mountains make haste;
In one movement I clear away all alarms to celebrate "Great Peace."

I am the commander in chief of the Great Han, Huo Qubing. I have received the order of the imperial palace for a punitive campaign against the Xiongnu, and I am currently drafting troops and buying horses in order to link up with the advance troops. Soldiers! Hang out the poster, and if there are persons who want to volunteer, quickly report their names.

(*Mu Lan enters in military dress and whipping her horse. Acts out descending from horse.*)

MU LAN:

(*Prelude couplet*)

Setting out on my trip to the battlefield,
I risk my life for the sake of the country.

(*Speaks:*) Anyone here at the gate? I have come to join the army.

ZHAO JING: (*acts out coming out and greeting her*) There you are! Report at the gate and enter!

MU LAN: (*acts out bowing*) Mu Shu reports for duty and enters.

(*The guards act out shouting in a threatening manner*) (*Mu Lan glances [left and] right, acts out assuming a respectful position*)

THE GUARDS: Commander in Chief, a young fighter outside wants to join the army and requests an audience.

HUO QUBING: Tell him to come in. (*Mu Lan acts out entering*) (*Huo Qubing gets on his feet and acts out observing her carefully. Acts out surprise.*)

HUO QUBING: You're such a handsome young man—you look just like a tender girl. What kind of courage and schemes do you have that you dare appear here before me, making light of a thousand trials? Soldiers, chase him away!

MU LAN: Just wait! (*Sings to the lead-in beat:*)

Commander in Chief, please sit down in your tiger tent,
And listen while I, Mu Shu, tell you a comparable case.
In earlier days, Chu and Han had many great generals,
But none measured up to that young man Zhang Zifang.[10]
  To this very day his portrait is seen in Lingyan Tower,
His face as handsome as that of some flowerlike maiden.
In commanding troops, all depends on tactics and strategy,
So how can one judge a person on the basis of his looks?
  How can one rashly judge the world's greatest heroes?
Please do not wrongly reject me, this young man Mu!

HUO QUBING: What capabilities do you have that you dare brag in such a manner?

MU LAN: Please listen. (*Sings as above:*)

You, General, are one of the pillars and beams of the state;
You will have your own considerations, your own ideas.
The Xiongnu basically are the leaders of nomadic tribes,
But for a long time they have troubled China on its borders.
  If we do not completely clean out their nests and burrows,
There never will be an end to the problems they may cause.
I, Mu Shu, consider myself a commander who can lead—
Unless I behead the king of Loulan, I will not return home.[11]

---

[10] Following the collapse of the Qin dynasty upon the death of the First Emperor, a civil war broke out among different contenders for the throne. The two final contenders were the hegemon-king of Western Chu, Xiang Yu, and the king of Han, Liu Bang. Eventually, Xiang Yu was defeated by Liu Bang, who was able to rely on the advice of many fine generals. His most important adviser was Zhang Liang (Zifang).

[11] Loulan was the name of a small kingdom in Central Asia in the second century B.C.E. that repeatedly fought off Han conquest.

HUO QUBING: Mu Shu, don't talk such nonsense! I will appoint you as a cavalry vanguard commander to test your capabilities. Mu Shu, listen to my orders. I order you to lead five hundred mounted soldiers and link up with Generalissimo Wei. In case of any failure or mistake, you will be punished according to military law.

MU LAN: Yes, sir!

HUO QUBING: All dismissed! (*All exeunt*)

(*Mu Lan enters, costumed as a soldier, together with four mounted soldiers*)

MU LAN:

(*Prelude couplet*)

Once I have the power to command,
I will give my orders to the many troops.

(*Speaks:*) I am Mu Shu. I have received the order of General Huo to cross the border for war and to link up with Generalissimo Wei. Officers! Our troops will depart for the steppe.

(*Backstage, music is played. Extras bring lance and horse, and Mu Lan acts out mounting the horse.*) (*They circle the stage three times, and exeunt*)

(*Extras enter again and line up sideways at the edge of the stage*) (*Mu Lan enters*)

MU LAN: What is the name of this place where we have arrived?

EXTRAS: This is the Bend of the River.

MU LAN: Then let's pitch camp right here. (*Extras shout "Yes, sir" and retire. Exeunt.*)

(*Mu Lan enters wrapped in a feather cloak, with extra holding a candle*) (*Acts out entering the tent*) (*Mu Lan holds the candle and looks all around. Extra exits unobtrusively. Mu Lan acts out rubbing her eyes and sleeping, acts out being startled awake, acts out heaving a sigh.*) (*Sings, to the level beat of flute and fife backstage:*)

Ah, who could have known
    That fate would be against us,
        That our country is suffering decay!
Unfeelingly
    I have abandoned
        My white-haired aged parents.
Removing hairpins and bracelets,

I've changed my dainty dress,
        Assuming the likeness of a man.
Alas, there was no one else
        To take my father's place
                And serve the country at the border.
For this reason,
        I carry lance and spear
                To give battle in front of the troops.
Leading these
        Five hundred men,
                I'll establish my fame on the steppe.

(*Acts out sleeping. Acts out being startled awake. Acts out heaving a sigh.*)

MU LAN: Just listen to the mighty flow of the Yellow River! How it startles my mind and moves my soul! (*Sings, to the level beat of flute and fife:*)

I hear the river's flow,
        Descending from heaven,
                And flowing toward my home village.
In dreams of my home village
        It still seems as if
                I am in my embroidery room:
Carrying plate and basin,
        Testing the water's temperature,
                I am waiting on my father and mother
                        With pleasant mien and fragrant dishes;
With Little Sister
        I play by the balustrade,
                Or buy flowers for my hair in the quiet alley.

(*Acts out sleeping. Acts out being startled awake. Acts out heaving a sigh.*)

MU LAN: This is an unprecedented joy for a woman, so why am I so sad and depressed? (*Sings, to the level beat of flute and fife:*)

If I can with
        The strength of my arms
                Capture the bandits, capture their king,
I will be able
        To command a large army,
                Dispatch troops and order the generals.

That will be for our
   World of women
      A first-time, fully unprecedented event,
And it will teach that
   Crowd of blushing stalwarts
      To deeply bow down before my toilette table.

(*Acts out getting up*)

MU LAN: Officers and men, where are you? (*Extras as mounted soldiers enter from left and right*) The sky is already bright, so let's break up camp and move on to link up with Generalissimo Wei. (*Exeunt*)

(*The khan of the Xiongnu*[12] *and barbarians. Wei Qing and Han soldiers. The two parties engage in a fierce battle. They fight three times for three rounds. Wei Qing is defeated. Exeunt.*)
(*The key to the whole play is found in this scene, so not the slightest slackening is allowed!*)
(*Mu Lan enters in a white coat and holding a lance*)

MU LAN: Here we have arrived at the foot of Mt. Rouge, so let me climb to a high spot so I can have a good look, to see where our General Wei is killing those rebels. (*Mu Lan acts out ascending the mountain and standing atop a high terrace. Backstage, the sounds of battle are produced. Mu Lan acts out being startled.*) In the distance, where dust is rising, I see defeated soldiers coming down, [like locusts] darkening the sky! Those must be the Xiongnu who flee in defeat. So let's go and fight them, so they will be attacked from both sides!

(*Wei Qing enters, fleeing in defeat, followed by the khan, who hotly pursues him. Wei Qing acts out giving battle and being defeated. Exeunt.*)

MU LAN: That's, that's, that's not good! How it is possible that we Han people are defeated by the barbarians? Let me advance and save General Wei! (*Acts out descending from the terrace*) (*Sings while music is played backstage:*)

Wait till I, this little Mu Lan, throttle those barbarians—
In a moment I will trample this steppe completely flat!
Don't mock me for being only a weak and tender girl—
Just watch me splattering this battle gown with blood!

(*Wei Qing enters, defeated. The khan pursues him, acts out fighting him. Mu Lan enters unobtrusively, acts out blocking and fighting the khan.*) (*The khan orders the extras to fight Mu Lan*

---

[12] Historically, the highest ruler of the Xiongnu was not designated "khan" or *kehan*, but *shanyu*.

from all sides. Mu Lan fiercely fights the khan in a man-to-man confrontation. The khan acts out being defeated and exits.) (Wei Qing turns around and comes out, and acts out expressing his gratitude to Mu Lan)

WEI QING: Who may you be, General, who just arrived? Allow me to express my gratitude for saving me.

MU LAN: I am Mu Shu of the cavalry vanguard under the command of General Huo. General, please pardon my crime of being late in linking up with you.

WEI QING: General, many thanks for saving me. Now please lend me a hand in exterminating these barbarians.

MU LAN: Yes, sir! I will immediately fight my way into their camp!

(Wei Qing and Mu Lan twirl their lances. Exeunt.)
(The khan enters, leading his barbarian soldiers)

THE KHAN: My children, you have seen how terrible these two *manzi* were.[13] They gave me such a beating that I couldn't get in a stroke, so what should we do now?

A SPY: The enemy troops have already arrived!

ALL: Check the situation out once again!

THE KHAN: In front of us there is nowhere we can go, and behind us the enemy comes in hot pursuit, so where can we flee for safety?

ALL: Let's fight them one more time to see who will be victorious in the end!

THE KHAN: So let's fight! Fight!

(Wei Qing and Mu Lan enter together. They engage in battle [with the Xiongnu] for a few rounds. [The Xiongnu] are defeated and exeunt.)

MU LAN: Where have we arrived?

WEI QING: We have already arrived in foreign territory.

MU LAN: General, we cannot slacken in our efforts. Let's pursue them closely and kill them till no single piece of armor is left!

---

[13] *Manzi* is a common derogatory term used by northerners for southerners. It may be used by northern Chinese to refer to southern Chinese in a rude manner. Here it is used by the Xiongnu to denigrate the Chinese.

WEI QING: You are right!

MU LAN: Please.

(*Together they twirl their lances and exeunt*)
(*The khan enters leading his defeated troops*) (*On the backdrop are displayed the signs of ocean waves*)

THE KHAN: My children, this place here is the Northern Ice Sea, so where can we hide ourselves?

ALL: We can hide ourselves on the icebergs for a while.

THE KHAN: At this moment we have no other solution, so let's cross the ice.

(*Act out stumbling and falling down on the slippery ice, and running away in order to escape*)
(*Exeunt*)
(*Backstage, the war drums are sounded*) (*Wei Qing and Mu Lan enter in pursuit*)

MU LAN: Where have we come now? How come we don't see even a single shadow of a barbarian?

WEI QING: We have arrived at the Northern Ice Sea. The barbarians must have been beheaded and killed to the last man by the Han troops, so I would propose to you, General, that we return with our troops and report to the throne.

MU LAN: I'm overjoyed! (*Sings to the level beat:*)
My teaming up with you, my general,
       Resembled the wind following the tiger,
       The dragon following the clouds,
             As together we went to the borders and secured the state.
Just look, from now on the cosmos is at peace,
And a unified globe now celebrates Great Peace.

WEI QING: Congratulations!

(*All act out shouting in support*) (*Wei Qing and Mu Lan twirl their lances. Exeunt.*)
(*Eunuchs and Emperor Wu of the Han enter*)

EMPEROR:

(*Prelude couplet*)

To seek revenge and wash away shame
Is the old ambition of a man of the Han.

(*Speaks:*)

Within the phoenix walls colored clouds rise above towers and pavilions;
Shrubs and trees are always in bloom, and both sun and moon are at ease.
The myriad countries, each in their costume, line up before the throne,
As the Son of Heaven of the house of Han rules the rivers and mountains.

We are Liu Che, the emperor of the Han dynasty. To Our distress the Xiongnu
have for years on end been troubling the Central Plain. Repeatedly We sought
to establish peace through interdynastic marriages, but that did not in the least
assuage the later problems. That's why the whole world shared in Our rage. We
ordered generals to lead Our army on an extermination campaign against these
barbarians to seek revenge for the people of the Han and wash away their shame.
Eunuchs, transmit Our orders: if any report arrives from the borders, inform
Us immediately!

(*Huo Qubing, with a red face and white beard, enters, holding his court tablet*)

HUO QUBING:

(*Prelude couplet*)

Red banners recently reported victory,
So I will thus inform my lord and ruler.

(*Acts out entering the throne hall*) (*Speaks:*) This old servant Huo Qubing reports to
Your Majesty: with the assistance of the valorous general Mu Shu, Wei Qing
recently annihilated the Xiongnu. These generals have returned to court and
request an audience.

EMPEROR: This is all thanks to your efforts as a chancellor. Let it be known
that We will see Wei Qing and Mu Shu, so We may reward and ennoble them.

(*Wei Qing and Mu Lan enter while performing the dance of obeisance. They act out entering the
throne hall and kneeling down.*)

EMPEROR: Please rise! You two have great merit in exterminating the caitiffs.
Please report your glorious achievements in detail.

(*Music is performed backstage. Wei Qing presents the register of meritorious achievements. The
emperor acts out reading it.*)

EMPEROR: Mu Shu has such great merits that he may be ennobled as a Marquis Within the Passes. Let him accept this reward and retire.

MU LAN: Please allow me a few words. (*Sings:*)

Your servant originally is
    Only a common citizen
        From the rustic countryside,
But to wield shield and lance
    In defense of Altar and Grain[14]
        Is the responsibility of a subject.
To exterminate the barbarians,
    And protect race and kind,
        Was the basic ideal of your servant;
I did not act on behalf of
    The Son of Heaven of the Han
        Or the dynasty of the house of Liu.
I did not aim for
    Great riches or high status,
        The ephemeral fortune of a moment;
Nor did I aim for
    My share of the spoils,
        And an idle fame that has no value.
I only request that our
    Sage and enlightened ruler
        Will retract the edict he pronounced,
And, as I lay down my commission,
    He will allow the bones of my body
        To return to my native hills and groves.

EMPEROR: Even if that may be your wish, how could We not properly distribute awards? General Huo and General Wei, please take the cap and girdle for Mu Shu with you.

(*The emperor and extras exeunt*)

HUO QUBING and WEI QING: Our congratulations, Marquis Mu! Tomorrow we will send Your Lordship off to his home village. (*Act out smiling. Exeunt.*)

Translated by Wilt L. Idema

---

[14] "Altar and Grain" renders the Chinese phrase *she ji*, which refers to the altar to the earth and the god of millet, symbols of the nation.

OUYANG YUQIAN

Mulan Joins the Army (1939)[1]

Act I

Characters:

MR. WANG

MR. LI

MR. ZHANG

MULAN

MR. ZHAO

CHORUS OF CHILDREN

MOTHER

FATHER

BROTHER

SISTER

MESSENGER

---

[1] This translation follows the screenplay as published in *Wenxian* magazine (Ouyang, 1939, pp. 1–31), with differences in the film version as noted.

Mulan dressed in male hunting attire, from the 1939 film *Mulan Joins the Army*.

(*Autumn. Clouds and trees. Leaves drop one by one onto the ground from the trees. A flock of wild geese emerges from the clouds. Close-up of bow shooting an arrow. Among the flock of wild geese, a goose is struck by the arrow and falls. When the bird falls to the ground, a horse rushes over and the rider bends over to pick up the goose. This is Hua Mulan, wearing pants and a jacket with a quiver on her back. She stops her horse. She puts the goose into her bag and again mounts the horse and goes. She speeds her horse far away. Mulan reaches a peak, stops her horse, and looks around. From among some bushes, there is a rustling, and Mulan draws her bow and shoots at it. Striking her target, she suddenly hears a cry of pain. It is in fact another hunter who had been concealed in the bushes. In pain he jumps up, sees Mulan, and recognizes her.*)

WANG: Ah, it's you, girlie!

(*Mulan is speechless in surprise. Another hunter comes out clutching at arrows; three others come out to ask after him.*)

LI: Wang, what were you calling out about again? Did you shoot something?

WANG: No, I didn't shoot anything; instead, I got shot by someone! Take a look . . .

(*He demonstrates to them where he was hit*)

ZHANG: Hey, isn't that a daughter of the Hua family?

(*Mulan rides over to the group*)

LI: That's right!

ZHANG: Pretending to be mad but actually scheming, she's come over to our village to hunt—and flaunt the rules!

LI: That's right!

MULAN: Big Brother Wang, I am truly sorry. I thought you were a rabbit. I didn't think you would have been crouching there.

(*Zhang instigates Wang*)

ZHANG: Wang, not only does she shoot you, she insults you by calling you a rabbit![2]

LI: That's right!

ZHAO: And she has the nerve not to acknowledge her "uncles"?

LI: That's right!

(*The men advance toward her and surround her horse, circling her menacingly*)

ZHAO: Hey, you stole something of ours. Quick, leave it here and we'll let you go.

MEN: Quick, leave it! Quick, leave it!

MULAN: Who stole something of yours?

ZHAO: What are you saying . . . you are from the Hua family village and have come over to our Li village to hunt. (*Mulan angrily gestures for him to continue*) That goose, that wild hen, and that rabbit were all raised in our village. You took them without asking; are you not a thief?

MULAN: That which flew in the sky and that which ran on the ground were taken outside this village.

ZHAO: Outside this village, huh? If you have entered our village gates you must pay a tax.

---

[2] "Rabbit" was Beijing slang for homosexual.

MULAN: When was this decreed?

ZHAO: Today.

LI: Right, this is a new regulation, made today.

(*Mulan pulls on her reins and tries to ride away, and the men block her path*)

MULAN: Let me go.

WANG: We have no problem letting you go.

LI: (*chimes in:*) Give us back all the game you killed.

WANG: Little Mulan, come down off your horse; we can have a chat.

(*Mulan tries to leave again and is blocked again*)

ALL THE MEN: We can have a little fun; we can have a little fun.

ZHAO: Little Mulan, don't be shy, we won't hunt you . . . just snatch you.

WANG: Little Mulan, little rider, if you're looking for a man, you've got me right here.

(*Mulan, outraged, tries to go again and is blocked this time by a pitchfork in her face*)

MULAN: If you still won't let me go, I will have to be rude.

LI: Little Mulan, don't get upset, I haven't married yet.

(*Mulan pulls on her horse, both angry and smiling*)

MULAN: Haha. Looks to me like you've all got a trick or two.

ZHAO: Have you only just realized that we men of Li village are all well versed in both literary arts and martial skills?

(*Close-up of Mulan*)

MULAN: Well, that part I just saw was the literary arts, right?

ZHAO: That's right.

MULAN: What about the martial skills?

ZHAO: As for martial skills, well, you couldn't handle it.

MULAN: How about we compare shooting skills?

(*Zhao grabs his horse whip and walks over to Mulan as he speaks*)

ZHAO: You want to challenge me in archery? Great! (*Draws arrow*) Do you see that [bird] flying in the sky?

MULAN: That is a wild goose.

(*Zhao uses his horse whip to point at the goose*)

ZHAO: I can shoot it with one arrow. If I say I will pierce its eye, then I will not pierce its mouth (*demonstrates with arrow tip on Mulan throughout this speech*); if I say I will pierce its mouth, then I will not pierce its leg; if I say I will pierce its middle, then I will not pierce its back (*whacks her on back with arrow to punctuate the last point*).

(*Everyone laughs together*)

MULAN: Sounds like your archery skills really aren't anything special; you should use just one hand, with the opposite shooting.

ZHAO: One hand? What kind of style is that?

MULAN: Take a look (*demonstrating*); open up the bow this way, lift up the arrow (*stretching her arm behind her back*), bring your other hand behind your back, and shoot that wild goose down from the skies.

(*Li takes an arrow in hand to try, without success*)

ZHAO: You shoot first and let us see.

LI: Right, if you succeed, we will let you go. If you don't find your mark, you and everything with you will rest here and your mommy will have to ransom you.

MEN: Good!

MULAN: Good. You have spoken, good sirs.

(*All the men grab their bows and arrows and try to copy Mulan's position*)

LI: A team of wild horses cannot make us go back on this word.

MULAN: Each of you, take a look (*points upward*). Wild geese are coming. I will shoot the first one in the row. (*As all the men stand apart, looking up, Mulan whips her horse harshly and rides off, to the men's dismay.*) Good-bye, all of you.

(*Zhao angrily watches her go off*)

ZHAO: We were tricked by this chick!

LI: That's right!

(*Close-up on the plentiful game that Mulan has caught, hanging from her sides. Pan over the city walls. We see her riding her horse against the slanting sun rays, accompanied by a group of young children, singing.*)

CHILDREN:

The sun comes out and fills the land,
The village children laugh. Ha! Ha!
Come on, come on, quick, come on.
Together we will hunt and admire the flowers.

(*Mulan sings along with them, innocently:*)

The sun comes out and fills the land,
With hard work we soon will copy her well.
If robbers and thieves come we will not fear:
All together we'll send them back home.

The sun comes out and fills the land,
In front of me lies my home,
Come on, come on, quick, come on,
Together we'll go ahead and share a cup of tea.

(*A voice from offscreen interrupts:*)

MOTHER: Mulan! Come back home!

(*Mulan stops and addresses the children*)

MULAN: My mother is calling me. She is certain to be mad at me for coming back late. Today I can't treat you to a cup of tea. Another day we will go together for a hunt, all right?

CHILDREN: All right.

MULAN: Well then, see you tomorrow! See you tomorrow!

CHILDREN: See you tomorrow!

(*The children leave*)
(*Mulan's mother stands at the house gates waiting for Mulan. Mulan dismounts from her horse.*)

MULAN: Mom.

MOTHER: Running wild all day long . . . how did you ever remember to come home?

MULAN: (*holds up her catch*) Mom, look!

MOTHER: I am looking. I wonder if what I'm seeing is or isn't a girl!

(*Mulan furrows her brow*)

MULAN: Mom, because Daddy was feeling better, I wanted to go out and catch some game to bring home, for him to get his appetite back.

MOTHER: Because you've been gone all day, your daddy has spent the day in a foul mood. Quickly sneak in from the back door and change out of those clothes before you go in to see Daddy.

(*Mulan hugs her mother*)

MULAN: My wonderful Mommy!

MOTHER: All right, all right, quick, go! Take your kill and hide it, too.

(*Mulan sneaks quietly around the back, leading her horse. She reaches the back door and ties up her horse, then goes to the well to get a drink of water for the horse. Then she picks up the game and sneaks through the back door. As she sneaks in, her father walks in to the kitchen.*)

MULAN: Daddy.

FATHER: This girl spends her whole day running wild outdoors (*mother and little brother enter*). Look at you!

(*At this time, her mother and younger brother come over*)

BROTHER: Sister!

(*The younger brother is Shulan; he runs over to his elder sister and tries to see what she is hiding behind her back. Mulan tries to shoo him away, but he pulls on her arm, revealing the goose.*)

BROTHER: Daddy, look at how much she got!

ELDER SISTER: (*from offscreen:*) Little Sister is back.

(*Mulan's elder sister walks in and, seeing their angry parents, looks afraid. Mulan's father addresses her mother, muffling his anger.*)

FATHER: I was frequently away at war. You see, look at how you've brought up your daughter.

MOTHER: But she also has never done anything bad; it's just that she loves to hunt. Who asked you to teach her how to shoot from the time she was a little girl, filling her heart with a love of playing in the wild? How dare you scold her now?

MULAN: (*crying*) It's only because Daddy was ill and with a poor appetite that I went out specially to hunt these for Daddy to eat.

(*Father's anger subsides somewhat, and [he] gestures at the animals*)

FATHER: These were all shot down by you?

MULAN: Of course they were all shot by me.

FATHER: I can't believe it.

BROTHER: I believe it. Sister is better at hunting than Daddy!

(*The elder sister quickly wags a finger at him and prevents him from saying more. Mulan gives Shulan a loving look.*)

FATHER: In the future you can't go out anymore.

MULAN: All right.

FATHER: Hurry up and change your clothes.

MULAN: All right. (*She starts to walk away*)

FATHER: Come back. (*He addresses her as if giving orders*) I am punishing you with three days of weaving a bolt of silk. You can't come out until it is woven perfectly.

(*Mulan bows angelically*)

FATHER: Understand?

MULAN: I understand, Daddy.

FATHER: (*hearing a sound*) Who's coming?

(*Mulan looks outside. An official messenger has arrived, delivering a document. Mulan's father greets him at the door.*)

MESSENGER: Is this the home of the honorable Hua?

FATHER: Just lowly me.

MESSENGER: (*taking out the document*) So it is you. There is an official dispatch for you.

FATHER: Thank you, brother.

(*He takes the letter and, from his chest pocket, takes out some silver to give the happy messenger a tip. Mulan, delighted, takes aim with her bow and arrow and shoots the messenger's hat off, just as he receives the coin. He cowers in terror. We can hear her little brother laughing. Mulan's father picks up the hat and pulls out the arrow, and there are two small holes in the hat. The messenger is very upset, and Mulan's father quickly pushes more coins into his hand.*)

FATHER: Just a little something for you.

MESSENGER: (*weighing money in his hand, smiles again*) You are too kind. (*He examines his hat in wonder*) What a good marksman! Good-bye, good-bye!

(*After he leaves, Mulan's father angrily rushes into the house, grasping the arrow. The family scurries away, and Mulan is the last to attempt to exit.*)

FATHER: You little good for nothing . . .

MULAN: You didn't believe that I was a good shot, so I wanted to give you a little demonstration.

(*Father moves to strike her with the arrow, and she runs out. Alone in the room, he looks at the arrow and smiles to himself, appreciatively. Then he looks at the envelope in his hand. On it is written "For the honorable Hua to break the seal."*)

FATHER: Something definitely is . . . something definitely is happening on the borders, and I am needed again to join the army (*he tears the letter open with the tip of the arrow in his hand*).

(*Interior. Mother and father are sitting alone together at the table in candlelight. Father is holding the envelope in his hand.*)

FATHER: Joining the army this time, it's not certain that I will return alive. You have to take care of all matters of the household.

MOTHER: You are so old, and you haven't recovered fully from your illness. How can you bear the difficulties of the battleground?

(*Cut to Mulan listening from her room, where she is weaving at the loom*)

MOTHER: How can you tell me not to worry?

FATHER: (*sadly*) Our country takes care of the troops for a thousand days in exchange for calling on troops when it needs them. Now that the country is in trouble, every civilian must go to war.

(*Mulan has stopped her weaving and is pressed up against the wall, listening intently*)

FATHER: How could I live off the country's support and just stay at home? That wouldn't do. I am not concerned about myself, but I only worry that there is no one to take care of things if there are problems at home. If only Eldest Son had not died, things would be different. But we have two girls . . . (*camera pans over sleeping younger son*) and with Shulan still so young, how could he take my place to join the army to prevent this old man from dying in some other land?

(*Mulan continues to eavesdrop*)

MOTHER: Eh, I just don't understand why they would come and attack us for no reason.

FATHER: They are bandits—what else is there to say?[3]

MOTHER: Truly, we have been married for twenty odd years . . . you were hardly ever at home . . . and the whole family relies on you . . . we might as well. . . . (*Starts sobbing*)

FATHER: Don't be sad.

(*Mother stops crying. They suddenly hear a sigh from the other room.*)

FATHER: Who is sighing out there?

MULAN: It's me.

FATHER: It's the middle of the night; what are you doing up sighing?

MOTHER: That child grows bigger by the day and is still not married . . . this is one of the things that weighs on my mind.

(*The sighing continues, and the parents cross the threshold. Mulan is still sitting crying, and her parents go in to talk to her.*)

FATHER: Child, why are you sitting here sighing, instead of working on your weaving?

---

[3] This and the line before it are not in the *Wenxian* script.

MULAN: Because of you.

FATHER: Because of me? Is it because I scolded you with a few harsh words today that you are angry?

MULAN: You should have scolded me; why should I be angry about that?

FATHER: Then what is it?

MULAN: Because in the other room you told Mother that you have to rejoin the army. I heard everything.

(*Father and Mother exchange looks*)

MULAN: I think you can't go.

FATHER: How can I *not* go?

MULAN: In your lifetime, you've been through dozens of battles. At your age, you should be at home, enjoying old age. (*She says bitterly:*) This year, you were also very ill. How could your body handle the icy wind and snow from the north? With Older Brother dead, and Little Brother still young, and Elder Sister about to marry . . . the whole family is relying on your guidance. As I see it, you mustn't go.

FATHER: A soldier's orders are firm like mountains, how can one not go? Fortunately, I am not that old, and I can still exert myself on behalf of my country. It's more glorious to die on the battleground than to die at home. (*He starts to cough*)[4]

MULAN: (*resolutely*) Father, I think . . .

FATHER: What do you think?

MULAN: I think I will go in your place to war.

(*Father, upon hearing this, jumps up*)

FATHER: What? *You* go in my place?

MULAN: Yes.

FATHER: How could that be?

---

[4] The section beginning with "and I can still" and ending with the coughing is not found in the printed screenplay.

MOTHER: Are you joking? How can a girl go to fight a battle? Go to bed!

(*Mulan continues to stand there*)

MULAN: No. Father taught me martial arts from the time I was a young girl; what use is that if I stay here at home? It would be better for me to go in Father's place to war. It would be first of all filial, and second of all it would be loyal, and when I return victorious people will realize: a girl, too, can bring glory to her home. "Dying on the fields of sand . . ." (*Father listens in disbelief*) "is my heart's desire." Father, please allow me to do this.

FATHER: I do appreciate your filial heart, but how can I let my daughter take my place under a false name?

MULAN: I can dress up like a man.

MOTHER: Bah! Everyone in and out of the village knows that you are a girl!

MULAN: Mother, Father, just tell everyone that I was always a boy and that, fearing I would not survive childhood, you dressed me up to pretend I was a girl. Now that I have grown up, I have changed back into a man and will take Father's place in the army.

FATHER: The officials will not accept that.

MULAN: Father is old and recently has been frequently sick. All he needs to do is explain the reasoning, and I will perform my martial arts moves to let them see . . .

(*Father seems to be slowly giving over to her argument*)

FATHER: Eh . . .

MOTHER: This won't do. This won't do.

MULAN: (*getting on her knees in front of her parents*) Father, Mother, allow me to do this.

FATHER: (*resting his hand on her head*) You are quite courageous. I cannot bear to stand in your way. But, going to battle is not good fun. When it comes to that time, you may regret it.

MOTHER: Pah!

MULAN: I may be young, but my conviction is deep. No matter the difficulty, I will not regret it.

FATHER: Good. (*He raises her to her feet*) Mother, go get my armor and let her put it on to see if it fits.

MOTHER: (*shakes her head*) I am not going.

FATHER: Then I shall go.

(*We see Mulan in military dress, practicing with spear and sword. Father looks happy and mother turns her back to them. Mulan walks up to her father.*)

MULAN: Father, what do you think?

FATHER: Looks to me very much like a very young man. But, what about your voice? (*Mother covers her mouth and laughs, and Mulan looks downcast*) Well, let's go to bed; we'll talk about it tomorrow.

(*Mulan practices deepening her voice to resemble a man's*)
(*Fade out*)
(*We see Mulan sitting gazing out her window*)

MULAN: (*in a deep voice, recites:*) "Wanting to serve this country with one's life, facing up to the dagger, cut off from loved ones." (*Outside, a rooster crows*) Kill!

Act 2

Characters:

FATHER

MULAN

MOTHER

WARD COMMANDER

BROTHER

SISTER

OFFICER HAN

LIU YING

ZHANG XU

YIN CI

MOTHER (OF ZHANG XU AND YIN CI)

(*Father enters, and we hear Mulan speaking offstage*)

MULAN: (*in her new, man's voice:*) General Hua, Mrs. Hua, I have a report for you.

FATHER: Who's there? Please, come in.

MULAN: (*bursting in, in full military dress*) I am Hua Mulan, paying respects to General Hua and his wife. (*Parents laugh*) Mother, Father, does my voice sound like a man's?

FATHER: It really does . . .

MOTHER: It may sound like it, but I really can't abide this.

(*From outside comes a voice, accompanied by the strike of a gong to announce the date of departure*)

WARD COMMANDER: Trouble rises on the borders! Everyone must come to join the ranks. Those who have been called must go forth in the next two days. If you miss the final date, martial law will deal with you. (*Goes on repeating, accompanying with gong:*) Trouble rises on the borders! Everyone must come to join the ranks. . . .

(*Mulan looks nervous, and the ward commander's voice fades away*)

MULAN: Good, I am going to go to a few market towns to buy a few traveling items.

FATHER: Good.

(*Mulan walks out, clearing her throat and practicing her man's voice as she goes*)

MOTHER: With her dressed up like this . . . she resembles our eldest son too much (*cries into her sleeve*).

(*Mulan walks into the marketplace, leading her horse, and picks up some bells*)
(*Back inside the house, her mother is readying her luggage, and her father stands in front of the window. Her sister and younger brother walk in.*)

SISTER: The food is ready.

FATHER: First bow to our ancestors.

(*The family goes together to the altar. Mulan lights a stick of incense at a candle and bows before the altar. She kneels before the altar.*)
(*At the dinner table*)

FATHER: A toast to favorable winds on your journey! Come back victorious after dousing the barbarians' fires.

MULAN: Thank you, Father, for teaching me the military arts. It will allow me to serve the country with loyalty and to help me fulfill my filial duty to you. Truly two perfect goals. This is the time to thank you; please do not worry about me (*drinks a cup to her father*).

MOTHER: Best wishes for your complete safety on this journey! I have never been separated from you once in your life.

MULAN: Mother, please don't worry about me, and thank you for permitting me to go. You have helped me to achieve my ideals and let me be a useful girl to our country. When I come back victorious, we will all have the comfort of being together again. Mother, just wait and you will hear good news (*drinks a cup to her mother*).

SISTER: Best wishes, Little Sister, and much success to you.

MULAN: Many thanks for your kind words. Take care of the home and serve Mother and Father. For those things I rely on you (*drinks a cup to her sister*).

BROTHER: (*also raising a cup to her*) Sister, if you aren't able to beat those guys, just write a letter home to me, and I will come right away to help you.

MULAN: Terrific, terrific! Listen to Mother and Father and study hard, and you will be able to serve your country well (*drinks a cup to her brother*).

(*Outside, the ward commander continues beating his gong and calling out. We see soldiers sadly taking their leave of their families while the messenger continues to call the summons to the soldiers.*)
(*We see Officer Han taking leave of his new bride sadly*)

WARD COMMANDER: Those who are joining the army, we depart today.

(*Liu Ying takes leave of his wife and baby*)

LIU YING: Daddy is going off to war now. Daddy is going off to war now.

(*He clowns around for the baby. He wipes a tear from his eye.*)
(*Two soldiers, Zhang Xu and Yin Ci, are bidding good-bye to their mother. The mother first turns to Xu and says:*)

OLD WOMAN: Little Xu, be careful out there with your bad temper.

XU: I'll pay no attention to anything, and pay attention only to killing.[5]

OLD WOMAN: Little Ci, you are always too lazy, always loving to sleep. When you go off to war, don't be as you are at home.

CI: Mother, don't worry. I will not sleep until I have won the war (*starts to yawn*).

(*Ward commander calls out again: "Those who are joining the army, we depart today . . ."*)
(*Mulan and her family are outside their home saying their good-byes*)

MULAN: I'll go now.

FATHER: Get on your horse.

---

[5] The second half of the sentence, beginning with "and," does not occur in the screenplay.

MULAN: (*to her mother:*) Your daughter's joining the army is a glorious thing. You should not be sad; you should be happy.

FATHER: That's right, we should be smiling to encourage her.

MULAN: Mother, smile. (*Mother smiles, with great effort*) Take care of your health, both of you. I am off.

(*Mounts horse*)

FAMILY: Take care.

(*The two old people weep. Mulan bows her head and cries.*)

FATHER: Take care, child (*as Mulan rides off*).

(*Fade out*)

Act 3

Characters:

MULAN

OFFICER HAN

LIU YING

LIU YUANDU

TEAHOUSE OWNER AND DAUGHTER

ZHANG XU

YIN CI

(On the road)
(Mulan goes forward on the road. Soldiers follow and then pass her, eyeing her. As each one passes her by, they each turn their head to appraise her. Though she is not afraid or embarrassed, she is very aware of them. Han and Liu ride by; the former thinking of his wife, the latter thinking of his children.)

HAN: I just brought home my new wife only sixteen days ago.

LIU: While you're gone your wife will surely find a nice young man to take care of her. But I . . . I have two plump and fair young children . . .

(Han is just about to curse out Liu when he notices Mulan coming from behind. Mulan approaches from behind and passes them. They stare at her with great interest. They wait for Mulan to pass by, gesture at her, and start to discuss her.)

HAN: Look, that fellow is quite fair.

LIU: Not only very fair, but a very tender morsel, too!

HAN: You haven't touched him; how can you tell he's tender?

LIU: What are you making eyes about?

HAN: I wonder what road this fellow is taking?

LIU: Let's watch him, and we'll go too and look for a little trouble.

HAN: Good.

(*They hurry to follow. Mulan enters a teahouse to rest; there are already several other soldiers there doing the same, seated on stools. There is a young hero, named Liu Yuandu, also sipping tea. He notices Mulan enter. Mulan also notices Liu Yuandu. Soldiers Han and Liu arrive and notice her. They go over to where she is sitting and lean toward her, circling her and hovering behind her. The tea serving girl brings Mulan a bowl of tea.*)

MULAN: (*accepting the drink*) Thank you.

(*The serving girl glances at Mulan and giggles, runs over to her mother and points out Mulan. The mother scolds her blushing daughter. Han uses his horse whip to tap Mulan on the shoulder.*)

HAN: Little brother, where are you from?

(*Mulan turns her head to look at him and slowly stands up*)

MULAN: I'm from Haozhou.

LIU: Where are you going?

MULAN: I'm going to Yan'an.

(*Han speaks in a mincing voice*)

HAN: What are you going to do there?

MULAN: I'm going to join the army.

LIU: It's several thousand miles from here. How are you going to get there?

MULAN: Why wouldn't I get there? (*Turning her head toward Han*)

HAN: There are robbers on the road there.

MULAN: I have my sword.

LIU: In the forest wild animals lie in wait . . . wolves and tigers!

MULAN: I can protect myself with bow and arrow.

(*Several men have gathered behind Liu and Han to listen*)

HAN: I advise you not to talk so big.

LIU: A little chicken like you! You would be a delicious tidbit for a wolf. (*The men laugh, with the exception of Liu, who stands up angrily*)

HAN: Hahaha. You really do look like a little chicken.[6] (*Mulan turns her head to the side. Han continues to speak, laughing.*)

HAN: Little brother, what is your surname?

MULAN: My surname is Hua.

HAN: You really do look like a flower.[7]

MULAN: You two, with all the current troubles around us, everyone is going forth to join the army: this is nothing more than serving one's country. There shouldn't be any countrymen bullying fellow countrymen. This is also the first time that we have met; how can you talk to me this way? Aren't you bullying me?

HAN: What a bad temper! How is this joking around considered bullying? (*He playfully swipes at her to hold her hand, and she grabs his arm and twists it behind his back. He squeals in pain, and the other men laugh at him.*) All right, you bastard, hands off!

(*Mulan walks off, without a care*)

HAN: Stop. Don't run off!

LIU: Sorry, we would like the honor . . .

(*Mulan has already gone out the door. She turns around and addresses them.*)

MULAN: OK, come and get me!

(*The two rush over to her. Liu Yuandu comes out to stop them.*)

YUANDU: Take it easy, take it easy. I just saw plainly that it was you two who were the bullies. I say you should forget about it; you shouldn't take grievances between you onto the battlefield. (*He walks toward Mulan*) You go on your way, you don't need to continue on with people like these.

HAN: Where did we dig up this guy? I advise you to stay out of private matters. This sword does not heed any man.

(*Liu Yuandu draws his sword, and Mulan stops his arm*)

MULAN: Brother, they won't give up. Just let me confront them. (*She removes some pebbles from her jacket*) And I'm not going to use my sword or spear, just these

---

[6] "Little chicken" (*xiaoji* 小雞) is homophonous with the word for prostitute or woman of easy virtue, *xiaoji* (*nü*) 小妓 (女); see also note I.

[7] Mulan's surname, Hua 花, means "flower."

few little stones. I'll let them see that I am not to be bullied. (*To the other soldiers:*) Come on.

LIU: Good! Come on.

(*They charge, with swords raised. Mulan throws the pebbles at them. Han's sword drops to the ground, his hand in pain. He cries out in pain. The same happens to Liu. They try to kick at Mulan and are struck by the pebbles in their legs. Mulan mounts her horse.*)

MULAN: Sorry, and good-bye.

(*She leaves an admiring crowd behind her. Yuandu also gets on his horse. The teahouse girl looks at Mulan admiringly.*)
(*The two tie up their horses at the next camp by the banks of the Yellow River. Mulan dismounts from her horse, and Liu Yuandu does so beside her. Mulan greets him. The two of them strike up a conversation as they walk toward the boarding house.*)

YUANDU: Those two guys were really hateful!

MULAN: (*laughing*) Thanks so much for sticking up for me.

YUANDU: It was nothing. Your martial skills are really impressive.

MULAN: You embarrass me.

YUANDU: May I ask your surname?

MULAN: (*Answers in a very friendly manner:*) I'm surnamed Hua. My name is Mulan. May I ask your name?

YUANDU: I am surnamed Liu, and my name is Yuandu. I am from Peiliang, and you?

MULAN: I am from Haozhou. Are you going to Yan'an as well?

YUANDU: Yes, are you?

MULAN: Yes, I am. My father is old and very ill, so I am taking his place to join the army.

YUANDU: Loyal and filial, both! How admirable!

MULAN: In matters of military campaigns I know very little, so I hope that I can learn from you.

YUANDU: Hardly. Let's take our rest at this inn here.

MULAN: Good.

YUANDU: Young man (*to the stable boy about his horse*), more hay.

SERVANT: Yes.

(*They enter the gates. They hear the approaching soldiers, who notice them. Liu and Han arrive and see Mulan there.*)

HAN: This must indeed be an apparition!

LIU: Or else a warrior spirit!

(*Mulan and Yuandu hear this and enter the inn, laughing. A large pot of boiling water is being prepared for the men to wash their feet.*)

INNKEEPER: Please sit, please sit.

(*Men are all washing their feet. They groan as they wash their feet. Mulan alone doesn't wash her feet. Zhang Xu notices Mulan and nudges Ci. They begin to circle her. Liu and Han try to get their attention and hiss for them to go over. Xu and the other men, hearing them, turn their heads and look over at Han and Liu. Mulan puts her hands in her clothes, and Liu and Han fear that she might have more pebbles in there. They call over Xu and others who walk over.*)

CI: What are you calling us over for?

HAN: That fellow is no softie. We have already suffered at his hands.

SERVANT: (*bringing bucket*) For you to wash your feet, sir.

MULAN: Leave it here.

(*Yuandu quickly finishes washing his feet*)

YUANDU: Brother Hua, I'm done washing up, come on over.

MULAN: You're too polite, too polite (*she picks up her bucket and goes into a private room*).

CI: (*very surprised*) What? He even has to go behind closed doors to wash his feet? (*He is shushed by Soldier Liu*) What?

LIU: He is a warrior spirit.

CI: A warrior spirit?

(*The moon shines on the Yellow River. Nighttime. We hear the sound of an* erhu[8] *accompanying a singing voice. The sky is filled with stars. An old man carries a little girl, who sings a Henan song.*)

---

[8] A two-stringed, bowed musical instrument.

Several people can be seen in the lamplight. Liu Yuandu and Mulan stand together outside beside the Yellow River.)

YUANDU: May I ask Big Brother's position in the army?

MULAN: I took my father's position, and that is of troop commander.

YUANDU: I am also a troop commander. We are of the same class, but considering Big Brother's military skill, you will certainly advance quickly in rank.

MULAN: *(smiling)* Thank you for your kind words. So long as I can fight on behalf of my country, position does not matter to me.

(Yuandu looks at her, nodding. The night watchman strikes the hour. Both yawn.)

YUANDU: Let's go to bed; tomorrow we have to continue on the road.

MULAN: You go first.

YUANDU: It is a rare thing for the two of us to have just met, but to feel like we are old friends. Who would have thought, one from Peiliang and one from Haozhou, suddenly in the same place. This must be predestined.

MULAN: We men would be friends anywhere; I would have met you wherever we went. Hahaha. See you tomorrow.

YUANDU: Tomorrow.

(He leaves for the inn, and Mulan watches him go and then stands alone, looking troubled. Sounds of water. She imagines her parents looking over her.)

INNKEEPER: Is there still someone out there? I am about to lock the doors.

(Mulan walks in)
(Interior. Mulan walks around the room and sees men asleep on their beds. As she would have to lie down with the men, she sits at the table instead. In the distance we hear the sounds of dogs barking and the song continuing. She props her head up and tries to sleep.)
(Fade out)

Act 4

Characters:

MULAN

OFFICER HAN

LIU YING

YIN CI

LIU YUANDU

MARSHAL

MILITARY COMMANDER

DEFEATED BARBARIAN GENERALS

BARBARIAN GUARDS

MARSHAL'S GUARD

WALL GUARD

(*Desert. All men are on horses and battling. Mulan stands out in battle, sweat rolling down her face.*)

(*Snow falls. We see flying flags and hear the sounds of drums and trumpets. Mulan's armor is covered in snow. She dismounts her horse and enters an inn.*)

(*Interior. Mulan walks in, passing a room where five other soldiers are seated around a table.*)

HAN: We've already been at the border and, without realizing it, it has already been three years. There hasn't been a single achievement. Now take a look at that Hua. We all joined the army together. He moved up in rank upon coming and is now the commandant.[9] I think he'll soon be promoted to chief commandant.[10] One more jump and he will be military commissioner.[11] Not only that, it seems to me that he has become beautiful.

LIU: That goes without saying. Everyone has exerted themselves in battle. Since coming he has won every battle; it's no wonder the general admires him.

CI: That guy is really strangely enchanting, almost as if he were a woman. I really don't know where he learned his military arts; how he manages to defeat the enemy is really puzzling.

HAN: It's a pity he's a man; if he were a woman . . .

LIU: What would you do?

HAN: (*lightly*) Why, I really wouldn't be able to take it! (*Everyone around him laughs at him, and he stands up*)

(*Liu Yuandu has entered, and everyone else stands*)

YUANDU: Where is Commandant Hua? Do you know?

CI: Commandant Hua has gone inside after returning from the field.

(*Mulan is inside grinding ink to write a letter. She writes, "Dear Mother and Father . . ." She is writing a letter home when Liu Yuandu calls her.*)

YUANDU: Commandant Hua, are you in your room?

---

[9] *Xiaowei* 校尉, a prestige or merit title for a military officer.

[10] *Jingwei* 京尉.

[11] *Jiedu shi* 節度使.

MULAN: Brother Yuandu, please come in.

(*Yuandu enters. He approaches Mulan.*)

YUANDU: Writing a letter?

MULAN: Tomorrow someone is going to Haozhou.

YUANDU: Sorry to bother you.

(*Mulan walks toward the fire and then back*)

MULAN: Not at all. Do you have some news?

(*Mulan faces the fire, and Yuandu walks over*)

YUANDU: We've received a secret dispatch. They are preparing an attack.

MULAN: Of course they are; they have suffered a few setbacks but will not give up.

YUANDU: But our military commander will not believe it.

MULAN: Looking at the circumstances, I think the blame lies with the military commander. His motives are very selfish.

(*The two drink tea and contemplate*)

YUANDU: True, but because of the victory in several battles, they will not consider this.

MULAN: I have a plan for attack . . . take a look at how this is written . . . here is an old battle map of my father's. In the past few battles, I have relied on this map. I don't know whether the military commander will trust my map; if not, I will die of anger!

YUANDU: Ah! But the most immediately important is to know where exactly the enemy troops are. We just need more evidence and the commander will surely be unable to protest.

MULAN: Good, we will go together to see the marshal.

YUANDU: What is your plan?

MULAN: We will summon up our courage and tell him that we wish to go out to spy on the enemy. Let's go.

YUANDU: Don't you have to finish your letter?

MULAN: The country is at risk—what are one or two letters to home?[12]

(*The marshal is sitting on a tiger-skin seat. The military commander enters.*)

MARSHAL: Commander, have a seat.

COMMANDER: Yesterday those two barbarian generals were questioned, and they truly have surrendered. They would like to meet with Your Honor.

MARSHAL: Good, let them come in.

(*The two enemy generals come in humbly*)

COMMANDER: Yes. The marshal's goodness and worth are known to all. (*He goes to door and shouts:*) The marshal will now see the defeated generals.

MAN: Yes!

(*The defeated generals enter and kowtow to the marshal*)

DEFEATED GENERALS: Your Honor.

MARSHAL: The two of you may rise. (*They rise, giving thanks*)

FIRST DEFEATED GENERAL: We minions have offended the heavenly lord. Your Honor's benevolence is so great, we are already ten thousand times blessed, and now we are honored with an audience.

MARSHAL: I am truly elated that you abandoned your leader (*the men grin ingratiatingly*), but I have heard that your kingdom's barbarian leader is planning to send forth troops to attacks us. Is there truth in this? (*The military commander gives the defeated generals a significant look*)

SECOND DEFEATED GENERAL: Our wretched kingdom, since having suffered so many defeats, is already without any power to launch an attack. That report of a coming attack is nothing but gossip.

MILITARY COMMANDER: It was just idle chatter.

MARSHAL: Please, Commander, take good care of these two.

(*Mulan and Liu Yuandu speak to the marshal's guard outside the marshal's quarters*)

---

[12] The last two sentences do not appear in the *Wenxian* script.

MARSHAL'S GUARD: The marshal is currently speaking to the two surrendered generals.

YUANDU: Who brought them in?

MARSHAL'S GUARD: They were brought in by the military commander.

MULAN and YUANDU: Oh no!

(*The military commander leads the two surrendered generals out from the marshal's chambers to his own quarters*)

MILITARY COMMANDER: Please come in.

(*The three enter the military commander's rooms, and they look around to make sure no one is around. They speak quietly to the military commander.*)

FIRST DEFEATED GENERAL: Our kingdom's khan has presented you with tens of thousands of gold pieces asking you to explain matters to the marshal. What need is there for concern? From now on, both our kingdoms will remain in peace.

COMMANDER: I showed good judgment.

(*Mulan and Yuandu drag the marshal's guard who guards his door toward them to discuss matters*)

MULAN: What if it is just a false surrender? Then what?

MARSHAL'S GUARD: (*looks to both sides, then replies:*) I also do not believe them. Please, the two of you wait a while, let me think something up. Let's wait until the military commander and those two have left, then we can go to the marshal.

YUANDU: All must use all their might to rescue us from danger.

MARSHAL'S GUARD: This is what we should do. (*He walks over to the entrance and looks inside*) The commander is coming (*Mulan and Yuandu quickly conceal themselves. The commander and the two surrendered generals leave, and the guard returns and brings Mulan and Yuandu toward the gated entrance of the marshal until he calls him in. He goes in and kneels before the marshal, who is being served tea and is reading a report*). Honorable Marshal, Hua Mulan and Liu Yuandu have some secret matters they wish to see you about.

MARSHAL: What other secrets can they have? You go ask them.

MARSHAL'S GUARD: They would like to speak about it to the marshal in person.

MARSHAL: Fine, call them in.

MARSHAL'S GUARD: Yes (*He rises and goes over to the door, gesturing for the two to come in*).

(*The marshal pleasantly watches them come in and sends the servant out girl with the tea*)

YUANDU and MULAN: Your Honor.

MARSHAL: What is it?

MULAN: (*Yuandu nudges Mulan to speak*) We have heard from a secret report that the barbarian kingdom is planning an attack and that their army is soon to come.

MARSHAL: This is all just gossip.

YUANDU: But there really is an army; it is not just gossip.

(*The marshal still does not believe them*)

MARSHAL: Well then, do you know where this large army is?

MULAN: (*after exchanging looks with Yuandu*) Since their movements have been completely secret, we thought that we would request that you order us to go ourselves to spy out their location.

MARSHAL: (*very confidently*) The military commander interrogated the two surrendered generals already, and we found that there would no attack.

YUANDU: What if those two were just falsely surrendering? Wouldn't that be a great mistake?

MARSHAL: (*very disgruntled*) Fine, let's not talk about this anymore. Go ahead, you are dispatched on a fact-finding mission!

MULAN and YUANDU: Yes, sir! (*They leave*)

(*Mulan enters her chambers with Yuandu*)

YUANDU: With the two of us going out to explore like this . . . won't people be suspicious?

MULAN: I think we will need to go in disguise.

YUANDU: In disguise as what?

MULAN: You can disguise yourself as a barbarian hunter.

YUANDU: And you?

MULAN: I . . .

YUANDU: Yes, it would be best for you to play a barbarian girl.

MULAN: Nonsense! How can I play a girl?!

YUANDU: Think about it, what would it matter if you played a girl?!

MULAN: I'm only afraid that I won't be able to look like one!

YUANDU: You?! Even not dressed up you . . .

MULAN: What?

YUANDU: Sorry, don't get mad . . . I'm going to go and change.

(*Yuandu and Mulan are dressed up as a barbarian hunter and girl and are now traveling in the desert with a camel*)

MULAN: Your costume is really quite good.

YUANDU: Certainly it does not compare to yours.

(*Mulan stumbles*)

YUANDU: Careful!

MULAN: Of course it's hard to walk, getting about in this getup.

YUANDU: With the way we are dressed, you know what we look like?

MULAN: Friends.

YUANDU: Not like friends.

MULAN: Brother and sister?

YUANDU: Yes, but people would think we are husband and wife.

MULAN: What?! (*Stops walking*)

YUANDU: Nothing.

MULAN: (*slightly angry*) This whole trip I haven't heard you say a single serious thing; you've been making jokes to no end. Let me ask you, are we on a serious mission or is joking around more important?

YUANDU: Of course work is more important.

MULAN: Do you just want to be like one of those muddled-up men who want to get caught out?

YUANDU: Of course not.

MULAN: Now your rank is lower than mine by a degree; I will command you: we will take separate routes. You go this way, and I will go this way. We will meet at the designated place. Hurry!

YUANDU: Yes, sir!

(*Mulan watches him go, smiling, and then sighs. Finally, she goes bravely in one direction. She enters the barbarian camps and looks around carefully. Two barbarian guards notice her and jump out.*)

BARBARIAN 1: Hey, where are you going?

MULAN: I am going back to my parents' home.

BARBARIAN 2: Where is your parents' home?

MULAN: Just over there, not too far from here.

BARBARIAN 1: Don't go any further. We'll go together to see our leader.

MULAN: I'm not going!

BARBARIAN 2: That's not up to you.

MULAN: I'm afraid.

BARBARIAN 2: Scared or not, you have to go.

BARBARIAN 1: Truly, it is strange to see a young girl here . . . how could we let you go?

MULAN: Where is your leader?

BARBARIAN 1: Just over there. (*He points it out to her, and she turns to look*)

MULAN: Is that an army over there?

BARBARIAN 2: Of course.

MULAN: With barracks like that, there must be several thousand troops!

BARBARIAN 1: Several thousands?

MULAN: What, there aren't?

BARBARIAN 1: There are at least several tens of thousands! They are definitely going to destroy the Tang army!

MULAN: What fun!

BARBARIAN 2: What fun? Enough of this, let's go.

MULAN: With the way I am walking? I can't run away from you!

BARBARIAN 2: I am afraid you'll run.

MULAN: You don't think that I'm all right? (*She puts an arm around each man's shoulder*)

BARBARIANS 1 and 2: Of course we do, of course.

(*Mulan acts flirtatiously toward them as she walks between the two of them*)

MULAN: It's better to walk this way . . . isn't this more fun?

BARBARIANS 1 and 2: Not bad!

MULAN: (*sings:*)
Two people walk together on one single road, ah,
You come too,
You come too, ah,
What is there for me to fear?

(*The two barbarians are smitten by this song, and Mulan takes the opportunity to knock their heads together. The two fall down, and she quickly pulls out her dagger. She stabs each of them. She sees that they are dead and quickly steals their clothing. She changes into their clothes and comes out from the brush. We hear the sound of horse hooves, and she looks in surprise into the distance. A young messenger rushes toward her on a horse; she checks that she is properly dressed and then runs out.*)

MULAN: Hey!

(*The messenger stops his horse and, looking at Mulan, sees her as one of his fellow soldiers. She walks in a barbarian manner and, waving her hands, calls to him. Unaware of her ruse, the messenger goes toward her. From her jacket, she pulls out her pebbles and holds them in her hand. When the messenger gets closer, she flings the pebbles at him, knocking him off his horse where she quickly runs forward to kill him. Mulan steals the missive that he has been carrying. Several barbarian soldiers see her and approach. She jumps quickly on the messenger's horse and rides off. She rides back to her barracks, wearing the barbarian clothing and riding the barbarian horse. She calls up to the wall.*)

MULAN: Open the gates!

(*The Tang army barrier guards mistake her for a barbarian and ready their arrows. She is nearly struck by an arrow.*)

MULAN: Stay your arrows! I am Commandant Hua!

(*The barrier guards are unsure whether to believe her*)

GUARD I: Why would Commandant Hua be wearing barbarian clothes? Eh, you say you are Commandant Hua, what identification do you have?

(*Mulan takes her papers out and puts them on an arrow, shooting them upward*)

GUARD I: This is really Commandant Hua; quick, open the gates.

(*Mulan rides in*)

Act 5

Characters:

MILITARY COMMANDER

SERVANT

MULAN

MARSHAL

(*The military commander signals to the surrendered barbarian generals. There are singing and dancing girls. The military commander drinks wine with the surrendered generals, all smiles. His servant enters in a hurry.*)

SERVANT: Sir, Hua Mulan has returned from his exploratory mission and has gone to see the marshal.

COMMANDER: What? He didn't come to see me first; how could he go directly to the marshal first?! Fine, let me go listen to what he has to say.

(*The two surrendered barbarian generals stand up too and exchange worried looks*)
(*The marshal sits on his tiger-skin-covered seat, and Mulan stands before him*)

MARSHAL: You came back today?

MULAN: Yes.

MARSHAL: What did you discover in your exploratory mission?

(*The military commander listens in from outside*)

MULAN: Many barbarian troops are coming; they are all hidden near a stronghold in the mountains. There are several hundred thousands of them. Their mounted troops are already about a dozen miles from our wall. There was a messenger that I killed . . . he carried this directive (*She presents it respectfully to the marshal*).

MARSHAL: Ah! What do you think?

MULAN: From my perspective, if we stay inside this wall I fear that if something happens there are too few of us. Further, within the wall, there are too many enemy agents. I fear that the barbarian soldiers within the wall are following orders from beyond the wall. It seems that we should send our troops into two detachments outside the wall to attack. We'll surround them from two sides and wait for them to come attack the wall. The wall will be empty, and they will try to turn around. We will then use our troops to break them down.

MARSHAL: Ahhhh.

(*The military commander emerges from behind the curtains*)

COMMANDER: This is the worst plan. Mulan, you say that there are many barbarian troops coming. What information are you relying on?

MULAN: I saw them with my own eyes.

COMMANDER: What did you see?

MULAN: I saw plentiful barracks, army horses, and provisions all collected in a nearby stronghold in the mountains.

COMMANDER: (*laughing*) I already knew that there were secret troops purposely sent to trick us into coming out from behind the wall. Our fortifications are strong. If we stay behind the wall to greet them, they will have no recourse. But if we come out from behind the wall, we will be falling into their trap.

MARSHAL: Here, I have a secret missive, taken from one of the barbarian troops.

COMMANDER: I, too, have gotten the same kind of letter, saying almost exactly the opposite.

(*Yuandu enters and approaches the marshal*)

COMMANDER: We can see that their schemes are very elaborate.

YUANDU: Your Honor, I followed your orders and went on an exploratory mission, and found that the barbarian troops are large, and that they are very close!

COMMANDER: Liu Yuandu did not wait for the marshal to summon him and just charged in. Doesn't he know the correct military rules? See him out!

(*Two men come to usher him out, and Yuandu continues to try to speak*)

MARSHAL: Yuandu, get out, first.

COMMANDER: Mulan, you are too young to understand matters and were tricked by the barbarians. You fell right into their trap and brought back the wrong message.

MULAN: I am loyally protecting my country from the heavens to the earth. Please do not slight a good person.[13]

COMMANDER: I have heard that you can also play a woman; is that right? Very well, how about you stop playing soldier and go sing the *huadan*[14] instead?

(*Mulan looks angry enough to strike at him*)

MARSHAL: Mulan, you had better withdraw for now; the commander makes a good point.

COMMANDER: With these juniors acting out of turn, it really is unseemly.

MARSHAL: It is commonplace that the young are looking to fight; it's best to just let them suffer a few setbacks.

(*Mulan enters her chambers angrily. Yuandu enters.*)

YUANDU: What happened today? I saw that the military commander definitely was trying to thwart us. I think he must definitely be taking bribes from the barbarians.

MULAN: I think he *must* be taking bribes from them.

YUANDU: What can we do now?

MULAN: I think on one hand we have to keep an eye on the military commander and those two surrendered generals and on the other hand get our men ready.

YUANDU: Ready for what?

MULAN: The way I see it, if a situation arises, you will have to take troops in secret beyond the gates and conceal yourselves. Within the city I shall stay to protect the marshal. Ah! See how our good efforts have fallen at the hands of these spies!

---

[13] This line does not appear in the *Wenxian* script.

[14] Role type of young, flirtatious heroine.

Act 6

Characters:

MULAN

LIU YUANDU

MARSHAL

MILITARY COMMANDER

MARSHAL'S GUARD

DEFEATED BARBARIAN GENERALS

BARBARIAN ADJUTANT

(*Nighttime with wild winds; the winds blow the banners and flags. Mulan is in the tower and looks up at the sky. A flock of geese passes by. Mulan turns her head and shouts.*)

MULAN: Yuandu, come quick!

YUANDU: What is it?

MULAN: Look at that flock of birds; it suddenly arose in a mass and flew over here. It must mean that the troops are approaching to attack the fortress now. Go beyond the gate and get ready. (*To the other men*) Commandant Wang, take a detachment of men north of the wall. Commandant Li, go west of the wall.

(*Barbarian mounted troops speed in. We see troops on foot proceeding forward and the feet of horses kicking up the sand. There are feet marching forward. Yuandu leads troops into hiding. The commander and the two barbarian generals are conferring. The commander nods his head. Mulan walks back and forth on top of the walls.[15] Liu Yuandu directs his troops to move forward. Fire breaks out within the walls.*)

PEOPLE: Fire! Fire!

MULAN: (*to her men*) Quick! Get down from the wall to put out the fire!

---

[15] Although unspecified, we may construe the walls as those of the Great Wall.

(*A large group of barbarian troops nears the wall. Sound of drums. Arrows and boulders rain down from the soldiers on the wall. The barbarian troops climb up the wall. We see barbarian troops falling to arrows.*)

(*The marshal surveys the situation, and the military commander runs forward*)

COMMANDER: Hua Mulan led the men to mutiny. I advise you to punish him.

MARSHAL'S GUARD: Nonsense! Clearly, it is the barbarians attacking us; how can you say that Mulan is rebelling?

COMMANDER: Those barbarians were brought here by him. Quick, there's still a way out at the north of the wall.

MARSHAL: (*disbelieving*) The barbarians attacked from the north; how can we still leave via the north?

COMMANDER: You are not listening to me! You will regret it too late!

(*Two soldiers capture someone setting a fire. It turns out to be the first surrendered barbarian general. A soldier kneels before the marshal.*)

SOLDIER: We caught one of those who started the fire. He says he wishes to see the military commander.

COMMANDER: (*drawing his sword as if to kill the barbarian general*) How can this be?! (*Tries to lunge forward, with sword drawn*)

MARSHAL'S GUARD: (*drawing his sword*) Hold on. Let's question him before killing him!

MARSHAL: So, after all, you had falsely surrendered. Why did you do it?

FIRST BARBARIAN GENERAL: Each has his own country—what else do you need ask?

MARSHAL: Why did you want to see the military commander?

FIRST BARBARIAN GENERAL: Don't you know? Because he could set me free!

MARSHAL: (*turning his head and addressing the commander:*) You said others were rebelling, but it was in fact you who was doing so. (*To the capturing soldiers*) Take them all to be executed.

(*The marshal's guard takes the captured general by the collar and pushes him out along with the military commander. Mulan rushes in.*)

MULAN: Honored Marshal, the barbarians have overcome us and are coming. Fortunately, we had made preparations, but even so we cannot hold the fort for long. Please, sir, quickly go to the south of the wall to lead the troops.

MARSHAL: Good. (*They leave together*)

(*At the gates of the district. The marshal mounts a horse. The second barbarian general, hiding behind a wall, shoots an arrow at him. The marshal is struck, and Mulan goes to him. The second barbarian general runs away.*)

MULAN: Quick! Grab the man who just shot that arrow. (*Two soldiers rush after him. Mulan addresses the marshal.*) Please, sir, get on your horse and go first to the south of the wall. (*The marshal does so in spite of the pain*)

(*People are running away in fear; one looks into the camera and shouts*)

MAN: The barbarians are coming!

(*Barbarians surge. Mulan and others send off the marshal.*)

MULAN: You, take care of the marshal and leave first. I have to turn back and fight this group.

(*The barbarians enter the marshal's office and empty chambers. The barbarian general laughingly sits in the marshal's seat, as his adjutant comes in to report.*)

ADJUTANT: Honored leader, within the city the Tang army is paltry; the greater part of them has left the city walls. I think they are going to block our way out of the city. We should quickly hurry out of the city walls and continue the fighting twenty or thirty miles out to finish the battle. Otherwise, I fear that we will be defeated here.

BARBARIAN GENERAL: (*carelessly*) You did not say this earlier, and look how easily we captured the city. If we retreat immediately, what would happen?

ADJUTANT: We didn't think of this strategy earlier.

BARBARIAN GENERAL: (*furiously*) No wonder people said you were dumb as a dog! Take all the treasures and the good-looking girls out of here. (*The barbarian soldiers rush around trying to gather as much as they can*)

(*As the barbarian general tries to get on his horse to leave the city, Mulan hurries over and kills the general. The rest of the barbarians run off in fear.*)

MULAN: (*shouting from horse:*) Their troops are in disarray! Quick, get them!

Act 7

Characters:

MULAN

MARSHAL

LIU YUANDU

(*The marshal's camp*)
(*Mulan stands beside the supine marshal, who is suffering greatly. He reads aloud from a document.*)

MARSHAL: I regret that I didn't listen to you. Let all the people know that I made a big mistake. My brave generals and officers courageously battled and were able to defeat danger to bring peace. Even in death I am pleased. (*Mulan sheds tears upon hearing this*) I have already reported to the emperor, to appoint Hua Mulan the new marshal. He is both loyal and brave, and well versed in strategy. He can easily take on this responsibility. You must all obey his orders; this is my dying wish. (*He takes a deep breath*) I ask your forgiveness. (*He dies, and all weep*)

(*Outside the camp everyone kneels in mourning. The marshal's flag with his surname "Zhang" is lowered and is changed to "Hua." Mulan mounts the platform as marshal. Yuandu enters the camp. The crowds bow to Mulan. Mulan addresses the crowds, with Yuandu at her side.*)

MULAN: I have been honored by our former marshal, and, further, the emperor orders that I take over as leader. You need not suffer any longer. The people need not be oppressed, nor flee from attackers, nor gain favor through nepotism. Spread my words afar.

GATHERED GENERALS: Yes, sir!

(*Fade out*)

Act 8

Characters:

MULAN

LIU YUANDU

YIN CI

(*Tang troops battling the barbarian troops in the snow. Mulan fights bitterly in the snow; Yuandu fights bitterly in the rain. Mulan kills barbarians. A barbarian on horseback falls in mud, and barbarians are seen being chased away by Tang troops. Mulan and Yuandu give chase on horseback and return with smiles of victory. They stand before a memorial stele on which is written "In the fourth year of the Great Tang, Hua Mulan quieted the barbarian troops." Mulan rides horse to high peak, and all the people bow to her.*)

GATHERED TROOPS: Congratulations, Marshal. You have achieved success in battle!

YUANDU: (*from horseback*) The marshal is virtuous in arts and war; he pacified the borders. Eternal glory to him for thousands of years and thousands of eras!

MULAN: This glory belongs to everyone. All I did was give orders.

YUANDU: (*smiling*) The marshal is too modest.

(*Mulan smiles at him. Everyone rides off. There is a party at night; all the people are dancing. Yuandu and Mulan stand together. Mulan smilingly accepts a cup of wine and drinks a few mouthfuls. We see a flag reading "Love the people like your children" and "Long Live Peace."*)
(*A group of children perform a masked dance. A goat is being roasted. Mulan and Yuandu drink together. All appreciatively watch a young girl perform a sword dance. Yuandu is drunk.*)
(*Mulan stands up and leaves; Yuandu quickly finishes his cup and follows her out. Mulan has already returned to her tent where she has removed her outer coat and has gone into her bedroom, feeling a little drunk. We can hear a little music from outside. She lies down on her bed, deep in thought.*)
(*Yin Ci helps Liu Yuandu go into his tent, holding his arm*)

CI: Old Liu, how did you fill your stomach with just a little wine?

YUANDU: I don't care . . . I'm going to go find the marshal.

CI: I think you had better go to sleep.

YUANDU: I won't sleep; you go to sleep.

CI: (*pulling Liu Yuandu back*) OK, I'll go, but you should be more careful, don't bother the marshal.

YUANDU: (*hiccups*) I know, I know. You think I don't know my own marshal's temper?

CI: *Your* marshal, that is funny! (*Exits, laughing*)

(*Yuandu drunkenly goes to Mulan's tent and sits on a rock outside. Mulan hears Yuandu's hiccuping outside, and goes out to see him.*)

MULAN: What is it? Are you drunk?

YUANDU: Ah, Yuandu is no more.

MULAN: Let me give you some good news.

YUANDU: What happy news?

MULAN: A letter arrived from the capital, saying that the emperor has summoned me to the capital. You will be promoted to remain here as commander in chief.

YUANDU: Congratulations to you.

MULAN: I congratulate you, too.

YUANDU: I don't want the promotion!

MULAN: Why not?

YUANDU: I want to spend my life serving you.

MULAN: That's child's talk! Go to sleep.

YUANDU: Yes. (*Mulan goes into her tent; Yuandu goes but then returns to the rock in front of Mulan's tent*)

(*Mulan from inside the tent sees Yuandu again. He is still sitting on the rock. Mulan laughs and goes back outside and stands behind him.*)

MULAN: Yuandu, what are you doing?

YUANDU: (*standing up quickly*) I am keeping watch here.

MULAN: Nonsense! When have I ever asked you to keep watch? I see you are really drunk!

YUANDU: I am not!

MULAN: Are you homesick?

YUANDU: No.

MULAN: Missing your wife?

YUANDU: I don't have a wife.

MULAN: Ah, yes, you haven't married yet . . . so you . . .

YUANDU: What is it, Marshal?

MULAN: You, go to bed, it's getting late. (*We hear the night watch struck*)

YUANDU: No.

MULAN: Go to bed. Tomorrow morning I will make a match for you.

YUANDU: I don't want that.

MULAN: Why not?

YUANDU: I've already got one.

MULAN: (*a little surprised*) Already got one? What is this girl's surname? Where is she?

YUANDU: I have her in my heart.

MULAN: Well, why didn't you marry her? I never said you couldn't take a wife.

YUANDU: I daren't speak to her about it.

MULAN: Why not?

YUANDU: That girl's temper is very bad, and her status is above mine. If I don't address her properly, she may well murder me!

MULAN: (*laughing*) Can there be such a case on earth?!

YUANDU: Yes, such a case exists on earth; do you think it's strange?

MULAN: You really are drunk, talking nonsense, and talking too much. Go off!

YUANDU: Yes, sir!

(*Mulan goes back into her tent, and Yuandu starts off and then stops again. She goes into the tent still feeling drunk and cannot get over a feeling of melancholy. In front of the table she practices some sword arts to try to distract herself from these feelings. While she is practicing her sword, she can hear music from outside. She sings along.*)

MULAN: (*singing:*)

Where is the moon?
The moon is in the chamber.
He shines inside my room,
He shines upon my bed,
Shines upon that shattered battlefield,
Shines upon my sweet ambition.[16]
When can I enter my beloved's bosom,
And speak my innermost feelings?

(*When she finishes singing, she can hear from beyond the tent Yuandu continuing the song. She looks outside.*)

YUANDU: (*singing from the rock:*)

Where is the moon?
She shines in her room,
She shines upon her bed,
Shines upon my shattered heart,
Shines upon my endless nights of restlessness.
When will she enter my embrace,
And I can speak my grieving heart?

(*As he sings, Mulan comes out to listen*)

MULAN: (*purposefully*) In the middle of the night who is out there singing?

YUANDU: Did the marshal not tell the people that tonight they should sing until dawn?

---

[16] *Huaibao* 懷抱 is translated here as "ambition" and below as "bosom" and "embrace."

MULAN: Ah, it's still you! Fine, go ahead and sing.

YUANDU: (*drunkenly*) Please, Marshal, feel free to give your suggestions!

MULAN: Hahaha, I don't understand!

YUANDU:

Where is the moon?
The moon is right beside me.
I have seen the moon's face.
(*Mulan is moved by these words*)
I brim over with the moon's light;
I gaze over facing heaven's edge.
I face heaven's edge and think . . .
I can't go crazy, yet go mad,
Turning my head, I see that it is you in the sky.

MULAN: (*moved*) Sung very well. We have been friends for twelve years already. Today I will teach *you* a song.

YUANDU: (*blushes*) The marshal is so kind. I could not repay it even with ten thousand deaths.

MULAN: Nonsense.

YUANDU: Yes!

MULAN: (*sings:*)

Where is the moon?
The moon is beside you.
You have seen the moon's face;
You have fallen for the moon's light.
Knowing that you have gazed, year after year,
Knowing that you have thought, day after day.
You needn't be anxious or hurried,
Turn your head, and there your Chang'e will have come down.

(*The two sing together:*)

MULAN and YUANDU:

You needn't be anxious or hurried,
Turn your head, and there your Chang'e will have come down.

(*Done singing, Mulan smiles widely*)

MULAN: Now you can go to bed.

YUANDU: Yes, sir.

(*Yuandu hurries off*)

Act 9

Characters:

EMPEROR

MULAN

LIU YUANDU

(*Emperor's palace*)

EMPEROR: Hua Mulan quelled the barbarians and succeeded over the threats at the borders, and for this I am very pleased. I have appointed Mulan to the Imperial Secretariat. Liu Yuandu has been appointed commandant of the Assault-Resisting Garrison.

MULAN: I was without great successes. I dare not accept the honor of the Imperial Secretariat. I only wish to return home to see my father and mother.

YUANDU: My skills are limited; from beginning to end I only followed the orders of Marshal Hua. This appointment is too high; I fear that I am not able to fulfill Your Highness' kind appointment.

EMPEROR: (*very pleased*) Hua Mulan is so filial to his parents, Liu Yuandu so loyal. I am very pleased! Each one will be given a sword and horse and six months' leave to return home.

(*The crowd cheers "Ten thousand years!" for the emperor, and the curtains are closed around him*)

Act 10

Characters:

MULAN

LIU YUANDU

MR. WANG

MR. ZHAO

FATHER

MOTHER

SISTER

BROTHER

(*Mulan's home. Mulan and Yuandu arrive on horseback. Mulan waves to everyone from her horse. Everyone greets her with smiles. The hunters Wang and Zhao are also there.*)

WANG: Marshal, Marshal, do you still remember us? (*Mulan, smiling, nods her head and goes on. Wang continues:*) That is my old friend.

ZHAO: Oh yes, I am also his old friend. We're old friends.

(*Mulan reaches her house. Father, mother, sister, and brother come out to greet her, as well as other neighbors.*)

MULAN: Father, Mother! (*She gets off her horse and goes in with her parents*)

(*She and the others enter the rooms. Mulan bids the two older people rise and she bows before them. The parents are smiling and crying simultaneously. Mulan turns to her sister and bows.*)

MULAN: Sister, all these years you were burdened. (*Her sister already has a child. Mulan rubs her younger brother's head.*) Brother, you have grown so tall!

FATHER: Go inside and change your clothes and rest a bit; we can talk later.

(*Mulan's mother goes inside with her, and her father addresses the crowd outside*)

FATHER: Everyone, please sit down in here.

(*Mulan goes with her mother to her old room, draws the curtains, and wipes the dust off the mirror*)

MOTHER: There's so much to say I don't know where to begin.

(*In the reflection in the mirror we see Mulan transformed back into a girl with flowers in her hair and women's clothing. Her mother presents her with a large handful of calling cards.*)

MOTHER: I don't know how many people have come to talk to you about a match; look at all the cards that have come for you. What are we to do?

MULAN: (*girlishly*) I have already chosen.

MOTHER: Already decided? What kind of person is it?

MULAN: Mom, first listen to his voice and *then* look at him, OK? (*Turns to the window and calls out:*) Liu Yuandu!

YUANDU: Here!

MULAN: (*laughingly*) What do you think?

MOTHER: Loud and clear.

MULAN: (*happily*) I'll take you to go take a look at him and see if he will do, OK?

(*She hurries to drag her mother out*)

MOTHER: Slow down; I can't be pulled along like this.

MULAN: OK, Mom, I understand.

(*Liu Yuandu is standing drinking tea when Mulan brings her mother out to point him out*)

MULAN: Brother Yuandu. (*He turns around*) This is he. (*To the gathered men*) Everyone, please be at ease.

(*Han looks at her in surprise. Liu Yuandu looks muddled. Ci and Xu look shocked. Mulan giggles and rushes out.*)

FATHER: What is going on here? (*Mother whispers in his ear*) Ah, I see what this is about.[17]

---

[17] The interaction between the mother and father occurs only in the *Wenxian* script and not in the film.

(*Mulan in bridal dress sits in a candlelit chamber. Yuandu joins her, dressed as the groom.*)

YUANDU: Where will you be hiding yourself tonight?

(*Mulan flirtatiously looks at him and smiles at her bridegroom. She falls into his embrace.*)

Translated by Shiamin Kwa

APPENDICES

APPENDIX 1

Summaries of Selected Pre-1949 Plays

Yong'en

A Couple of Hares (Shuangtu ji)

Written by Yong'en. Not listed in earlier bibliographies. The fourth play of the *Four Plays of Ripple Garden* (*Yiyuan sizhong*).

This play was composed during the Qianlong period (1736–1795). The "original incident" is found in the *yuefu* folk song "Poem of Mulan" of the Northern Dynasties period, and in Xu Wei's *The Female Mulan Joins the Army in Place of Her Father* (*Ci Mulan tifu congjun*) of the Ming. This play was written by expanding on Xu's play. It has forty scenes and consists of two parts.

During the Northern Wei there lives a student by the name of Wang Qingyun (style Sixun), who hails from Quni. He has been engaged since childhood to the daughter of Chiliarch Hua of the same district. Because he has failed the examinations, he feels frustrated and depressed, and therefore leaves home to visit friends. Suddenly, he sees an apparition of Guanyin, who in the blink of an eye changes into a Diamond Warrior, but he cannot figure out what that might mean despite all his efforts.

Chiliarch Hua's name is Hu, and his style is Sangzhi. His wife is lady Jia. Their eldest daughter is Mulan, who has just turned sixteen. She has studied the martial arts with her father and is well-versed in all techniques. Mulan has a younger brother and a younger sister, but they are still little children. Mulan keeps two hares, one male and one female, but it is impossible to figure out which one is which. One day, as she is spinning by the door, she suddenly sees an apparition of Guanyin in the clouds, who then changes into a Diamond Warrior. Guanyin announces to Mulan that she will be "greatly recognized." Mulan reaches the following understanding:

> A woman's shape is transfigured into the body of a man
> And a man will later become a woman!

The great king of Black Mountain, Bao Zipi [Leopard Skin], is plundering the region of the Yellow River, causing great hardship to the common people. The khan sends out military registers, hoping to draft five thousand crack troops in Hebei. The district magistrate recommends Hua Hu for service. At the behest of the district magistrate, the two battalion commanders Mo Qianzhu and He Rugu, carrying the arrow of command of Xin Ping, the commander in chief for the campaign against the west, go to the house of Chiliarch Hua Hu to offer his congratulations and to appoint Hua Hu as the commanding general for the region. It just so happens that Hua Hu is not at home. When Hua Hu returns home and learns of his military appointment, he is very concerned. Hua Hu is over sixty years of age, his strength is failing, and he cannot obey the order. When Mulan sees how advanced in years her father is, she decides to change from her female dress to male attire and to join the army in place of her father. Mulan tells the family servant:

> If I do not become the most exceptional woman of my age,
> I will have lived this life in vain!

Mulan eagerly makes her preparations by buying a sword and lance and a fine horse. The neighbors bring wine and food to the Hua home to see her off. The servant informs Hua Hu of Mulan's decision and preparations. Hua Hu is both surprised and ashamed, and he strongly urges Mulan to abandon her decision to join the army. But Mulan has already made up her mind and swears she will go, so Hua Hu can do nothing else but accept her decision. In male attire, Mulan joins the army as the son of Hua Hu. He Rugu and Mo Qianzhu fail to see through her disguise, and when they see the apparition of Guanyin changing into a Diamond Warrior, they do not understand its meaning. Mulan swears an oath, which goes:

> My loyalty and filiality depend on this day;
> My valor and courage can be compared to those of any man!

When Wang Qingyun learns that Mulan has joined the army, he is filled with admiration, so he loves her only the more, and he makes up his mind to wait until Mulan returns home from the campaign in order to marry her. Hua Hu urges Student Wang to find another wife, but the latter is unwilling to do so, and Hua Hu realizes that Student Wang is an extraordinary man.

Vanguard Commander Niu He is a greedy and lustful man, who is equally interested in men and in women. As soon as he has fallen in love with the handsome features of Hua Hu (the assumed name of Mulan), he wishes to have sex, but he is met with an absolute refusal and therefore carries a grudge against Hua Hu.

When the troops have been camping at Gubeikou for half a year, Commander in Chief Xin Ping has still not arrived. The Hua family sends a servant to the army to take Mulan padded clothes and a letter. When Commander in Chief Xin Ping arrives, he orders the troops to advance. Vanguard Commander Niu He is greatly defeated and only escapes with his life when Hua Hu single-handedly comes to his rescue. The commander in chief demotes Niu He and elevates Hua Hu to the rank of vanguard commander.

Xin Ping deploys his troops and officers and orders Hua Hu and his troops to trick the enemy by feigning defeat. The Great King of Black Mountain indeed is taken in, and when the troops lying in ambush rise on all sides, he suffers a great defeat with many losses. Niu loses his life on the battlefield.

When Bao Qianjin, the younger sister by a different mother of the Great King of Black Mountain, hears how handsome Hua Hu is, she falls in love with him. She then orders her elderly maid to change into male dress and go to Hua Hu's tent in order to deliver a secret letter, in which she promises to collaborate on the inside for a common attack on Black Mountain. At this moment the two armies have already been locked in struggle for eleven years. Just when Xin Ping is filled with worry because he still has not been able to subdue the enemy, it is reported that Hua Hu requests an audience. Hua Hu reports Bao Qianjin's plan. Xin Ping follows Hua Hu's advice. Without hesitation he grabs this opportunity and inflicts a great defeat on the enemy. When Hua Hu attacks, he captures alive Bao Zipi and his younger brother Bao Jiuguan. The army returns victoriously, having accomplished its mission after a total of twelve years.

When the Son of Heaven of the Northern Wei gives out awards on the basis of merit, Xin Ping is appointed chancellor, and Hua Hu is appointed secretarial court gentleman. The other officers also receive their rewards. Hua Mulan declines any official appointment as she wishes to return home to wait on her parents. The Son of Heaven admires Hua's filial piety and awards the hereditary rank of vice general to the Hua family.

Wang Qingyun learns from a border report of Mulan's merit in battle and visits the Hua family to offer his congratulations.

Hua Mulan takes her leave of Xin Ping and leaves a letter with him in which she explains how she had served in male guise for twelve years. When Xin Ping reads the letter after she has left, he is filled with even greater admiration for Mulan. He reports the matter to the emperor, and the latter shifts her appointment to Wang Qingyun. Wang Qingyun becomes a secretarial court gentleman, and Hua Mulan becomes a lady of the first rank. Hua Hu receives a second rank noble title, and lady Jia becomes a lady of the second rank.

On the way back home, Mulan sees the couple of hares she had kept since childhood running toward her to welcome her. Her younger brother whets a knife and slaughters a pig and a goat to prepare a welcoming meal for his elder sister. When Mulan meets with her parents and siblings, sadness and joy intermingle. She gives five hundred taels of silver to He Rugu and Mo Qianzhu. Mulan changes into female dress, and when she comes out to see them, they are utterly flabbergasted: they had been together for twelve years but never realized that Mulan was a girl.

The Hua family receives the imperial edict: they are covered with glory and everyone is filled with joy.

This play is preserved in a wood-block edition printed by the mansion of Prince Li [Yong'en] of the Qianlong period.

Summary by Zhang Guofeng, in Li Xiusheng, 1997, pp. 554–5.

Chen Xu (1879–1940)

Hua Mulan (1897–1914)

Hua Mulan from Shangqiu has lost her mother at an early age. Her father, Hua Hu, served at court in a military function and reached the rank of chiliarch. But because he had submitted a critical memorial that displeased the emperor, he was dismissed, whereupon he returned to his home village. He is still alive but is already more than fifty. Mulan has a little brother called Yao'er and a little sister called Munan, but both of them are still very young. Because the family is very poor, they rely exclusively on Mulan, who weaves night and day in order to provide for the family's needs.

When the khan crosses the border on a southern campaign, the emperor issues an edict summoning soldiers to block the enemy. The officials and village heads check the population registers, and every able-bodied male will have to join the army. When Hua Hu falls ill, Mulan weaves a piece of brocade that very night and orders Yao'er to go to the market and sell it, so that they will have the money to cure the father's disease. Yao'er runs into their neighbor Lin Shou, a sixty-year-old seller of herbs, who is getting ready to join the army; he gives the medicine to Yao'er.

The military rolls list Hua Hu's name, but Yao'er keeps that information from his father. Hua Hu is filled with desire to protect the country and display his loyalty, so he can only hand the books he has written on military matters to Mulan, hoping that she will study them and teach them to her brother and sister.

Murong Yude, the richest man in Shangqiu, has been smitten by Mulan's beauty. In order to be able to execute his plans, he wants Hua Hu removed so he can lay his hands on Mulan. He sends a letter to the authorities in which he recommends Hua Hu for a command in the army. Hua Hu is appointed as commander of infantry and cavalry. Twelve missives are sent down, and the village head calls on him to depart for war. Mulan dresses herself as a man and puts on the armor her father used to wear; she studies the military books and practices the martial arts, until she is prepared to join the army in place of her father. She passes an inspection by Hua Hu, who sees that she has a full understanding of military matters, and accepts Mulan's request that she join the army in his place. He also practices the military arts at home with his daughters and his son. On horseback Mulan wields bow and arrow, sword and lance, and all kinds of weapons, displaying her extraordinary abilities. Hua Hu submits a memorial to the throne, stating that his son Mulan will substitute for him and lead the army into battle. The emperor issues an edict in which he grants his permission and appoints Mulan as commander in chief for the pacification of caitiffs. Heading the troops drafted in Shangqiu, she is to depart for Yanshan.

Cen Jian and other "good fellows of the green forests," infuriated by the disparity of riches and the corruption in official circles, want to volunteer "to serve the king." In order to stock up on supplies, having learned that Murong Yude is the richest man in the area and spends money like water, they go and rob him that night. With five thousand strong men and supplies worth a hundred thousand cash, Cen Jian and Guan Tianxiong volunteer to join the army and place themselves under the command of Hua Mulan.

Mulan takes pity on the elderly in the army because of their suffering and orders that all people forty years and over be allowed to leave. By this action she wins great popular support. Mulan takes her leave of her father, brother, sister, and neighbors. On the parade grounds she organizes her troops, and, following an inspection of infantry and cavalry, she divides her troops into twelve battalions and gives the order to depart for the north. During the twelve years of her campaign, reports of Mulan's victories arrive without interruption, and her family members and the neighbor Lin Shou are overjoyed. Mulan sends a letter from which her relatives learn that her troops are victorious wherever they arrive, that she has already crossed the Yellow River and reached Yanshan, and that she will return with her troops once she has defeated the enemy for good.

From Zuo, 2005, pp. 122–3. This summary is based on the text of the sixteen-scene play published in Shenbao *in 1914. A number of acts were published as early as 1897.*

Mei Lanfang and Qi Rushan

Mulan Joins the Army (1917)

Hua Mulan hails from Yan'an. Her father's name is Hu, and she has one sister and one brother. Her younger sister's name is Muhui; her little brother is still a toddler. Mulan has an extremely filial character. She loves martial arts; when later she is instructed by Hu, her knowledge is doubled.

At this time the world is in chaos. Chinese and barbarians are at war with each other. Battles are fought continuously, with no end in sight. Right then the Turks rebel, and the court orders He Tingyu to lead the troops in a punitive campaign. The village head collects the soldiers on the register to go to the front and join the fighting, and Hua Hu's name is also listed in the register. But Hu is advanced in years and without strength, incapable of carrying a lance.

Mulan sees how worn with age and decrepit her father is—he definitely is incapable of storming ahead and joining the battle. But to serve as a soldier is a duty of the people, and when it comes to exerting oneself on behalf of the state, there is no distinction between men and women; instead, each should exhaust his or her natural function. If one fearfully hides oneself away, accepts the dispositions of one or two powerful people, only loves one's village and only cares for one's children, refusing even to make an effort as light as pulling out a hair, then on what can the state rely with this type of people? But if the state collapses, there will be many things that will turn out to be impossible, even though one would like to enjoy one's private pleasures within the circle of the family! Mulan considers that, even though she is a woman, her only solution in these troubled times, now that her father is too old and her brother too young, is to go on the campaign as a substitute for her father. This is not a contrived emotion or a false ambition—she hopes to achieve the reputation of a filial daughter and also to make some contribution in order to stimulate those weak-spined men who cling to life. She thereupon requests permission from her parents to go and fight as a substitute for her father.

She serves in the army for twelve years and never displays her original nature. Repeatedly she establishes great merit. When the army returns victoriously, she refuses an official appointment and goes back. Upon her return home, she goes to her own room, discards the military outfit, and once again is a girl!

This summary appeared in Gujin xiju daguan *(Zhongwai shuju, 1921), and was reprinted in Dong, 2003, p. 118. A summary of the same play, based on a preserved manuscript titled* On Campaign in Place of Her Father *(Daifu zheng), was printed in Zeng, 1989, pp. 358–9.*

On Campaign in Place of Her Father (*Daifu zheng*)

When the Turks conduct a raid across the border, He Tingyu is appointed as commander to repulse the enemy, but in successive battles he is defeated again and again. He urgently dispatches people to the region of Yan'an to draft troops. A certain Hua Hu, who lives in Shangyi Village, is listed in the military registers. Because this man is quite advanced in years, his daughter Hua Mulan decides to take on the false guise of a male and to join the campaign in place of her father.

As soon as Mulan approaches the battlefield, she sees a general falling down from his horse and immediately rushes forward to save him, to realize only when she comes up close that it is Commander in Chief He Tingyu. During the campaign Mulan repeatedly establishes great merit, and very soon she is promoted to the rank of general.

One night, as Mulan is making the rounds, she notices that the birds above the enemy camp are flying up in fright. She deduces from this that the enemy is preparing a surprise attack that night. She has her troops hide themselves in anticipation, and the ambushed Turks suffer a decisive defeat. The Turks do not dare violate the border again, and He Tingyu returns to court victorious. He praises Mulan's merits, and she is appointed secretarial court gentleman. Mulan does not accept her appointment, refusing her office and returning to her home village.

After twelve years of separation from her family, she and her relatives are finally reunited. Because Mulan did not accept her appointment, the court now orders He Tingyu to reward her with rich gifts. When He Tingyu arrives in Shangyi Village and goes to see Mulan, she comes out to greet him in changed dress. Only now does he realize that she is no man. Even more surprised and impressed, he hurriedly returns to the court to ask for appropriate titles and rewards.

The above summary is based on a copy kept at the Beijing Municipal Drama Research Institute. For the original incidents, see chapter 56 of the *Historical Romance of the Sui and the Tang*.[1] The text was composed and performed by Mei Lanfang and Qi Rushan.

---

[1] This appears to be a mistake. The play more likely derives from *A Couple of Hares* by Yong'en.

A revised version of this script was produced by the modern playwright Ma Shaobo.

Mulan Joins the Army

During the Northern Wei, the Turks conduct a raid across the border. Commander in Chief He Tingyu leads his troops to meet the enemy. Because their military strength is weak, he drafts the officers and troops who had already retired from the ranks and tells them to hurry to the border regions and together stop this foreign humiliation. The name of a certain Hua Hu is listed in the military registers, and when he receives the summons to join the army, his daughter Mulan is weaving at the door. The military missives arrive one after another, and Mulan is deeply concerned that her father, too advanced in years and burdened by illness, lacks the strength to go on a campaign. Moreover, the family lacks a man of suitable age to be drafted. She thereupon decides to join the army in place of her father. Hua Hu initially is unwilling to give his permission and only assents once Mulan has persuaded him with gentle words. Mulan thereupon takes on the false guise of a male and uses the name of her younger brother Muli. Crossing the Yellow River and fording the Black Stream, she hurries toward the border. When Mulan and her men arrive on the battlefield, Commander in Chief He Tingyu is surrounded on all sides by Turkish troops. Only when Mulan and her troops join their forces with He's troops do they succeed in breaking through the double encirclement, and Mulan repeatedly establishes great merit. After twelve years, He Tingyu and his men finally succeed in crushing the Turks. On the eve of the army's return, Mulan requests permission to return home and nurse her wounds. When she arrives back home, her father's hair has already turned white as frost. When they see each other again, joy and sadness are intermingled. He Tingyu is ordered by the king of the Wei to reward Mulan with titles and gifts—he also intends to give his daughter as bride to Mulan. When He Tingyu arrives at the Huas', Mulan comes out to see him in changed dress. Only then does he realize that she is a girl.

[This summary is based on the] edition printed by the Baowentang in Beijing. Revised by Ma Shaobo. Performed by Du Jinfang and Li Huifang of the Zhongguo jingju yuan.

For another adaptation of the same play produced and printed in the early 1950s as A New Mulan Joins the Army *(Xin Mulan congjun), see Zeng, 1989, pp. 360–61.*

Pifu

Joining the Army: On the Road (1932)

A One-Act Play with Arias

Mulan is on her way to join the army in place of her father and is traveling along the high road with a family officer. As the family officer gazes on Mulan, he is overcome by emotions and heaves a sigh:

> This country for these last few tens of years;
> These mountains and rivers for thousands of miles. . . .
> The Xiongnu have taken up arms,
> And if one day their troops cross the border,
> They may well, carried on by their victories, arrive at the Phoenix Gate!
> Rarest of all is this woman who campaigns in place of her father,
> Shaming to death all those many men!

While Mulan is walking along with the family officer she is also observing the great landscape, and she is deeply moved. The family officer asks her: "Young lady, you are an upper-class girl and have spent your life hidden away in the inner apartments. Now you arrive here, in this world of ice and snow. Just look: the earth has cracked and the rocks are broken, and all plants and trees have shriveled. How can you bear this?" Mulan replies: "Since ancient times those who live in the inner apartments would not leave the gate, but how can the past be a model for the present now that the country is in chaos? Look at these rivers and mountains like embroidered brocade—in the blink of an eye they may turn into foreign territory. So why talk about 'upper-class'? I am afraid I will then be trampled like all others!"

While they are talking the hour of dusk, when tired birds return to their nests, arrives. The two of them come to a village, where they find some empty rooms to stay for the night. When the family officer sees how desolate the place is, he warns Mulan that there might be evil people around, so they'd better move on. But Mulan does not agree with him: "We who join the army should see it as their first duty to remove bullies and bring peace to the common people, so why should we fear evil people?" Mulan goes to sleep, and the family officer keeps watch. When he discovers Wang Qiang and Chen Xiang, two robbers who steal from the rich to give to the poor, he loudly calls the alarm. Mulan wakes up and confronts the robbers. She steps up to them and advises them in loyal words: "Now the country is in chaos, the king employs robbers and capable men.

If you are willing to risk your life on the battlefield, burn your mountain strongholds and follow me in joining the army. . . . Sacrifice yourself for the sake of the poor! How can you bear to bring harm to your compatriots, relying on your martial skills and sharp weapons that kill people?" The two robbers Wang Qiang and Chen Xiang are moved by Mulan's sincere and loyal words and declare: "Sir, you are a man who is determined to save the country. How would we dare disobey your good words? Allow us to be your grooms, so we can pay you back for your enlightening advice." So on the road to joining the army, she acquired two more heroes.

Summary based on text in Wenyi zhanxian *30 (17 October 1932), in Dong, 2003, p. 569.*

Ouyang Yuqian

Mulan Joins the Army (*a* Guiju) (1942)

The interregnum between the Sui and the Tang. Hua Mulan from the Hua family village in Yan'an Prefecture, while out hunting, passes by the Zhang family village. When some young bullies create trouble for Mulan, they are defeated by her. (Scene 1)

Grasping the opportunity of a civil war between the Sui and the Tang, Khan Hali raises a million troops to invade the Central Plain, aiming to clean out the Jiangnan area. (Scene 2)

At noon, Mulan enters [her home], carrying the game she has shot. Her mother tells her to weave silk, but Mulan's thoughts are on saving the country and saving the people. The village head brings the military order telling Hua Zhifang to join the army that very day as he has been drafted, in order to block the advance of the foreign country. Mulan's father has fought in the army all his life, and he is also advanced in years and beset by illness, so Mulan proposes that it would be best if someone replaces him. As her little brother is still too young, Mulan dresses as a young military officer and requests to join the army in place of her father. Her father teaches her how to use the lance. (Scene 3)

An inn on the bank of the Yellow River. Hua Mulan and other people on their way to join the army are drinking wine. When Wang Si and Zhou Pao try to take advantage of Mulan because she is still so young, Liu Yuandu is filled with indignation. Mulan hits an "iron horse"[2] hanging from the eaves with a stone

---

[2] Windchimes.

pellet, and all are overawed by her skill. Wang Si and Zhou Pao ask to become her students, and with Liu Yuandu they plan to travel together to Yan'an to join the troops. Wu Cheng arrives at the inn escorting the prisoners Li Yuanhui, Huang Sheng, Zhang Biao, and Zhao Rulong. While he himself drinks merrily he doesn't care whether these condemned men live or die. Mulan steps up to him and intervenes, and she also gives money to provide the prisoners with food. She also urges them to fight the enemy. When the others have fallen asleep, Liu Yuandu and Mulan make small talk, but she does not allow him to raise personal matters. (Scene 4)

Khan Hali leads his barbarian troops on an attack across the Great Wall. When he learns that the commander in chief of the border passes has died, he continues toward the Central Plain. (Scene 5)

When Mulan and her companions run into scattered troops and refugees, they learn that the commander in chief has died. Wu Cheng wants to kill the prisoners and run for his life, but Mulan saves the prisoners. The prisoners volunteer to follow her to the border pass to fight the enemy, but Liu Yuandu suggests that they return to the pass in the second line of defense to collect the dispersed soldiers. Mulan lays out their strategy, and all swear to follow her even into death! (Scene 6)

The barbarian troops march toward the second pass. (Scene 7)

At the pass of the second line of defense, Liu Yuandu has collected five thousand troops, and Li Yuanhui has brought in the army supplies. All agree to appoint Mulan as general. Mulan gives her orders to her troops in preparation for the enemy attack. The barbarian troops are foiled by the "empty city trick"; when they do enter the gate, they are surprised by the soldiers lying in wait. Mulan hits Khan Hali with a pellet on his left thigh, but he manages to escape. (Scene 8)

Mulan's parents are concerned about Mulan. Mulan has a letter-goose[3] deliver a letter, in which she tells them that she has led the troops in battle, and the emperor has appointed her as commandant to guard the border passes. (Scene 9)

The enemy has increased its troops. Mulan increases discipline, as she wants her army to win the final battle. When Mulan and Khan Hali meet on the battlefield, he hits Mulan in her thigh with an arrow after a treacherous shot. Liu Yuandu and Li Yuanhui save Mulan from danger. (Scene 10)

---

[3] A messenger bird.

When Mulan and her companions arrive in front of a hill, Mulan wants them
to return and fight the enemy, so she uses all her strength to pull the arrow out,
whereupon she faints. Liu Yuandu returns to block the pursuing enemy, while
Li Yuanhui dresses Mulan's wound. Khan Hali and his troops search for Mulan;
but, he is led away from her by Zhang Biao and his fellow prisoners. Despite her
wound, Mulan observes the battle, and by beating the drum she boosts morale,
fighting off the enemy. (Scene 11)

Mulan sleeps in her tent, where two maids are waiting on her. Liu Yuandu and
Li Yuanhui, who both have been wounded, come to see her. Ever since he dressed
her wound, Li Yuanhui has been aware of the true situation, and these last few
days his mind has been in a daze, so he leaves under the pretext of doing the
rounds of the camp. Liu Yuandu does not understand why Mulan only wants
to be served by maids and does not allow him to come close. But when he hears
Mulan's sighs in her tent, he realizes that she is a woman in male disguise, and he
becomes even more loyal to her. When Mulan wants tea, he enters, bringing her
some tea, but Mulan tells him that in the future he is not allowed to enter her
tent unless called for: he'll be beheaded if he goes against that order! (Scene 12)

The local elders arrive with gifts for the troops. Mulan urges her officers to
protect the state. It just so happens that the enemy troops are tired and short
on supplies, so Mulan orders the army to counterattack. (Scene 13)

The barbarian soldiers long for home and their morale is at a low. A spy reports
that Hua Hu has died and the Tang troops are retreating. Khan Hali orders his
troops to pursue and kill them. Mulan, in the disguise of a blue-faced devil, meets
Khan Hali on the battlefields. She leads him to a dead-end valley, where he is
thoroughly defeated. (Scene 14)

Khan Hali leads his troops as they flee for their lives. Mulan leads her troops in
pursuit. (Scene 15)

Soldiers and civilians celebrate their victory over the enemy, and Mulan proposes
to inscribe the commemorative stele with the four characters *Zhonghua shengli* [China
Victorious]. (Scene 16)

In front of Mulan's tent. After twelve years of battle, Wang Si and Zhou Pao
have become somewhat disappointed. When Mulan, having had some wine, returns, she is overcome by loneliness. Liu Yuandu feigns drunkenness to test her
feelings, by saying that he is in love with a girl but does not dare speak to her.
Mulan tells him not to act improperly—in due time a Chang'e will descend from
the sky for him. (Scene 17)

Wang Si and Zhou Pao meet with Li Yuanhui. Li Yuanhui wishes to spend the rest of his life on the border. (Scene 18)

Mulan's family welcomes her back home. A matchmaker arrives to arrange a marriage for Commander in Chief Hua. Wang Si and Zhou Pao also ask the matchmaker to arrange matches for them. (Scene 19)

Mulan is making her toilette in front of the window and narrates to her father how she conducted affairs. Mulan's father brings Liu Yuandu in and tells him that the commander in chief wants to arrange a marriage for him. From behind a curtain Mulan tells him that she wants her cousin to become his wife, but Liu Yuandu refuses. When Mulan appears from behind the curtain, she asks him whether he recognizes her. Only then does he recognize Mulan. Mulan and Liu Yuandu are married and become a happy couple. (Scene 20)

From Dong, 2003, p. 1260. The summary is based on the edition of the play in Ouyang, 1980, vol. 2.

Translated by Wilt L. Idema

APPENDIX 2

Mulan in Three Novels of the Qing Dynasty

*The story of Mulan is not only narrated in a cluster of chapters in the hundred-chapter His-*torical Romance of the Sui and the Tang, *but also gave rise to two independent novels. Each of the following summaries is translated from the* Zhongguo tongsu xiaoshuo zongmu tiyao.

Chu Renhuo

Historical Romance of the Sui and the Tang

Synopsis of Chapters 56–61

Liu Wuzhou [a Chinese contender to the throne after the fall of the Sui] strikes an alliance with Heshana Khan of the Turks [Western Tujue] to invade Jinyang and Kuaizhou. The khan conscripts an army. Hua Hu's name figures in the conscription list, but he is already old, so his daughter Mulan dresses up in male garb and joins the army in his stead. Among Liu Wuzhou's men is a valiant general, Yuchi Gong, who fights fiercely against Qin Shubao [a valiant general of Li Shimin, the future Tang Taizong], but neither side wins a decisive victory over the other. The two men engage in a strength contest. Yuchi Gong uses Qin Shubao's mace to strike three times at a large boulder, breaking it in two, but Qin Shubao achieves the same effect on another boulder with only two strikes of the mace. Liu Wuzhou suspects that Yuchi Gong has ulterior motives, and he demotes him to Jiexiu to be in charge of fodder. Xu Shiji manages to defeat Liu Wuzhou with a stratagem, and Liu Wuzhou seeks refuge with the Turks, but he is killed by Heshana Khan. Yuchi Gong switches his allegiance to the Tang. Heshana Khan is defeated by Dou Jiande's troops. Just at the moment of extreme danger, Hua Mulan comes to his rescue and manages to save him, but is captured herself by Dou Xianniang [Jiande's daughter]. Among the other prisoners is also Qi Guoyuan, who comes from Luo Cheng's headquarters carrying a letter in which Luo Cheng asks Qin Shubao to ask Shan Xiongxin to act as a matchmaker and arrange a wedding between Luo Cheng and Dou Xianniang. However, Qi Guoyuan has been captured on his way by the khan and made into a cavalry soldier. Dou Xianniang, hearing that Mulan is a filial daughter who has joined the army in place of her father, is filled with admiration for her and retains her as a personal attendant. She also gets hold of Luo Cheng's letter. Later, the prince of Qin, Li Shimin, defeats Wang Shichong and captures Dou Jiande and Shan Xiongxin. Wang Shichong is discarded as a commoner. Dou Xianniang and Mulan go to meet Li Shimin carrying knives in their mouths, to show their wish to be executed instead of their fathers. Empress Dowager Dou commends the girls' resolution. She acknowledges Dou Xianniang as a niece and bestows lavish honors upon Mulan, sending them back home. Dou Jiande is also pardoned. He shaves his head and becomes a monk. Shan Xiongxin is executed. Qin Shubao, Xu Shiji, and Cheng Yaojin each slice a piece of their thighs to roast as a sacrificial offering to Shan Xiongxin. Moreover, Qin Huaiyu [Qin Shubao's son] and Shan Xiongxin's daughter Ailian are betrothed.

Dou Xianniang goes back home and attends the burial of Empress Cao, moving her residence to the side of the grave. Mulan also returns to her home province, after being entrusted by Dou Xianniang to deliver a letter to Luo Cheng. When Mulan returns home, she finds out that her father has passed away, and that her mother has remarried. When the khan hears of this, he selects Mulan for the imperial harem. Mulan then entrusts her sister Hua Youlan with the delivery of Dou Xianniang's letter to Luo Cheng. Thereupon, Mulan slits her throat and dies. Hua Youlan, who has donned male clothes to carry out her mission, reaches Youzhou. Luo Cheng soon recognizes her true gender and tries to sleep with her, but Hua Youlan resists firmly. Eventually, she and Dou Xianniang will both marry Luo Cheng. Shan Ailian and Qin Huaiyu also get married.

Zhongguo tongsu xiaoshuo zongmu tiyao, 1990, p. 423.

Anonymous

The Story of the Loyal, Filial, and Heroic Mulan.

Also known as *The Story of the Wondrous Maiden Mulan* (*Mulan qinü zhuan*).

Also known as *The Complete Story of the Wondrous Maiden Mulan* (*Mulan qinü quanzhuan*).

(thirty-two-chapter novel; c. 1800)

Synopsis

The novel tells the story of a Zhu Ruoxu, who lives in Shuanglong Garrison [*zhen*], Xiling District [*xian*], Guangzhou Prefecture [*fu*], Huguang province, during the

Sui dynasty. Zhu is by nature extremely filial and of peaceable disposition. Because Yang Su, prince of Yue, and Yuwen Huaji, the grand mentor, have arrogated power to themselves, Zhu repeatedly fails to qualify for the prefectural examination. Only when Yang Tingchen is appointed as magistrate of Xiling is Zhu summoned for a personal interview, as a result of which he is selected as the top candidate in the district and sent to the prefecture for further selection. However, the prefectural magistrate Wang Jiu has long been on bad terms with Yang Tingchen, so he has the latter arrested on the false charge that he has recklessly selected bogus scholars. When Dou Zhong, a fellow candidate [of Zhu's], sees the accusation, he is enraged and raises a rumpus in the courtroom. Dou Zhong happens to be the brother of Dou Jiande, military commissioner of Kaifeng, and Dou Jianwen, attendant gentleman of the left in the ministry of personnel of Heir Apparent Shaobao. When Wang Jiu gets to hear the full story, he is left with no choice but to let Zhu go to the capital as a candidate.

Li Jing of the Li family village in Jingzhao Ward [*xiang*] is poor but upright. One day, while on his way to Luoyang to visit some relatives, he encounters a dragon god and marries two dragon maidens. The dragon maidens, seeing that Li Jing is of utmost sincerity and uncalculating mind, hand down to him the secret texts on the technique of "evading stems" [*dunjia*]. Afterward, Li Jing, having failed to win over Wu Yunzhao, throws in his lot with Yang Su. Yang Su's concubine Hongfu elopes during the nighttime with Li Jing, and the two of them subsequently seek refuge in Taiyuan. Li Jing spends five years in Taiyuan, during which he devises three plans on behalf of Li Shimin and then returns to Chang'an. He pays a visit to Yang Su, bringing with him a fine steed and a bejeweled sword to ask for forgiveness. Yang Su has Li Jing build a following of clients.

While going to the capital, Zhu passes by the temple of the Goddess of Smallpox. The goddess enlightens him through the combined teachings of Daoism, Buddhism, and Confucianism, and Zhu loses interest in pursuing an official career. He reaches the capital just at the time when Yangdi has murdered his father and killed his brother. He goes to visit Li Jing and acknowledges him as his teacher. Li Jing hands down to him the secret texts on the evading stems technique, whereupon Zhu takes leave to return to his hometown. At Zhuxian Garrison he meets with Yuchi Gong, from Mayi District in Shandong, who sells his writing skills for a living. The two become sworn brothers, and Zhu recommends Yuchi Gong for appointment and sends him to the capital to meet Li Jing.

In Chang'an Li Jing recommends Yuchi Gong, Wei Zheng, Fang Xuanling, Qin Jing, Chu Suiliang, Cheng Zhijie, Changsun Wuji, and others to Li Shimin. As a result, Yuchi Gong serves as military adviser, Wei Zheng assists as preceptor to the emperor, and Fang Xuanling serves as assistant in the establishment of schools. Thus, the Taiyuan administration improves with each passing day. When Yangdi travels south to Yangzhou, lingering there and forgetting to return, all the noblemen of the empire take possession of their provinces and commanderies. Li Jing then secretly returns to Taiyuan.

Zhu, after returning to his hometown, practices meditation every day with monks, nuns, and Daoist adepts. As a result, his granddaughter Zhu Mulan, who is not yet ten years old, is thoroughly versed in all the doctrines of the Three Teachings, Mind-to-Mind Transmission, and the Sublime Dharma. At that time, Grand Mentor Wu Jianzhang is killed for disobeying a decree. His son Yunzhao leads an army to attack Nanyang, but he is defeated by Han Qinhu. He then becomes a monk and assumes the Dharma name "Sangwu" [Mourning for the Self]. Zuiyue [Drunken Moon], the abbot of Guanyin Monastery in Shuanglong Garrison, invites Sangwu to preach the Dharma in his monastery. At that time, Mulan, who is just ten years old, is fully able to sustain a conversation with Sangwu. When Zhu is about to die, he hands down to Mulan the occult books on the "evading stems" technique. After his death, the house is burnt to ashes by a fire. The household is entirely supported by the two women's and Mulan's needlework.

Soon after, the Sui dynasty comes to an end and the Tang dynasty is established. Yuchi Gong, duke of Guo, carries out the imperial order to build the walls of Wuchang. The project has just finished when he is again ordered to repair Xiling Monastery. Yuchi Gong, to show gratitude for Zhu's assistance, recommends that Zhu's son Tianlu be put in charge of the local battalion [*difang qianhu*]. He also recommends Tianlu's brother Tianxi as prefect of Changsha, and Yang Tingchen's son Yan as prefect of Wuzhou. Mulan practices horse riding, archery, and military training every day in addition to spinning and weaving. With the guidance of Sangwu, Mulan masters all seventy-two weapon techniques. A thousand-year-old fox spirit teases Mulan, but she injures one of its legs with the precious sword presented to her by Sangwu, and the fox spirit disappears.

Taizong plans to wage a campaign against the Turks. He appoints Yuchi Gong as generalissimo, and Li Jing as army supervisor. Yuchi Gong conscripts soldiers in Huguang for the northern campaign, and he promotes Zhu Tianlu to be in charge of the cavalry. However, Zhu Tianlu suddenly falls ill, so Mulan dresses up in male garb and joins the army in her father's stead, fulfilling her duties both as a filial daughter and as a loyal subject. Mulan meets Yuchi Gong and Li Jing, and together they reminisce about the past. Mulan is enfeoffed as general of Wuzhao. The great army is soon deployed. On their march [to the frontier], they pass by Wutai Mountain. There, Mulan pays a visit to Sangwu's friend, the Daoist Jingsong, who presents her with a wise camel. This is like adding wings to a tiger.

When the Chinese army reaches Jiebei Pass, Ebao, who is in charge of guarding the pass, immediately sends the signal for help. The king of the Turks appoints Xiehe as generalissimo, and Kanghe'a as army supervisor to fight against the enemy. Mulan takes Wulang [Five Wolves] Pass with a stratagem and captures Li Chen, who is in charge of guarding the pass, and Xiehe.

The war continues like this for ten years, during which the Tang army is only able to take one pass and two commanderies. Taizong issues a decree to demote Yuchi Gong and Li Jing to commandant [*houjue*] in order to urge the army to fight a more successful campaign. The king of the Turks also issues an edict, to recruit worthy advisers. The thousand-year-old fox spirit that had been injured by Mulan has now transformed into the great immortal Dushou, who is appointed as army supervisor. Through his magic arts he repeatedly defeats the Tang army. However, Mulan is able to defeat his sorcery with the magic talisman of the Daoist master Tieguan [Iron Cap], and [she] breaks into Yumen Pass. The generalissimo of the Northern Barbarians is killed, and the vice general is captured. The king of the Turks declares himself a subject of the Tang and surrenders to China.

Mulan returns in triumph. Passing by Wutai Mountain, she once again performs obeisance to the Daoist master Jingsong. Jingsong invites Mulan to see the Confucian master Wu Dagao, who expounds to her the doctrine of Confucius and Mencius, the principles of humaneness, justice, rites, and wisdom, the virtues of filiality, brotherly love, loyalty, and trust. Thereupon, Mulan is awakened to the truth. After returning to court, Mulan receives titles of nobility, and she is appointed as attendant gentleman of the left in the Ministry of War. When Mulan is summoned to the capital, she submits a memorial to express her true feelings, in which she reveals that she is a woman and does not wish to move to the capital. Taizong then enfeoffs Mulan as princess of Wuzhao and confers on her the imperial surname Li. He also bestows titles upon her parents and brothers. Later on, Mulan's parents both pass away, and she engages in earnest self-cultivation while also raising and educating her small brothers. Taizong once again summons her to the capital, but Mulan sends a second memorial to express her feelings, in which she begs the emperor to allow her to observe mourning for her parents and take care of her brothers.

Later, Taizong pays heed to the malicious rumors spread by Zhang Changzong and Xu Jingzong, to the extent that great chaos will surely come from those who carry the surname Wu, that is to say, the Wuzhao general Mulan. Therefore, Taizong summons Mulan to the capital for the third time with the intention of killing her. Mulan submits a third memorial to express her feelings, in which she expresses her loyalty and chastity, and to prove her sincerity she cuts open her chest with a sword [and dies].

Taizong is filled with remorse. He changes Mulan's title to "chaste and heroic" princess and inscribes her memorial arch with a plaque that reads "Loyal, Filial, Courageous, and Heroic." Mulan is buried at the foot of Mulan Mountain. After Wu Zetian has ascended the throne, she bestows the title of Empress Zhaolie on Mulan.

Zhongguo tongsu xiaoshuo zongmu tiyao, 1990, pp. 673–4.

Zhang Shaoxian

An Extraordinary History of the Northern Wei: The Story of a Filial and Heroic Girl.

(forty-six-chapter novel; 1850)

Synopsis

The novel tells of He Hu, chief bandit of Black Mountain during the reign of Tuoba Gui (386–409) of the Northern Wei. He Hu gathers 100,000 people in order to usurp the power of the Northern Wei. The counselor in chief Wulühe personally sponsors the grand commander in chief Xin Ping to be appointed as generalissimo and the vice commander in chief Niu He to be appointed as vanguard. Together, they lead an army of twenty thousand, which sets forth to exterminate the enemy. They also carry the imperial order to draft commoners into the army to take part in the campaign.

In the Hua family village of Hebei commandery, Hua Hu, a former battalion head, has long lived in retirement. His elder daughter, Mulan, who is just seventeen years old, has been betrothed to Wang Qingyun, the son of Assistant Instructor Wang from the same village. However, the wedding has not yet taken place. Hua Hu's younger daughter, Munan, is only nine years old, while his son, Jiao'er, is only five. The district head puts Hua Hu's name at the top of the conscription list and orders him to join the army without the slightest delay. Mulan, knowing that her father has attempted several times to put an end to his life, is in constant distress night and day. She then orders her maid to buy clothes and a horse in order to join the army in her father's stead. Her parents will not hear of it, but when Mulan takes out her sword in order to slit her throat, they give their consent. Mulan therefore joins the army, assuming the name of her father and, together with Mo Qianzhu and He Rugu from the same commandery, she crosses the Yellow River and reaches Gubeikou.

Mulan displays great prowess while performing military exercises on the training field. She is appointed as commandant by the generalissimo Xin Ping, and she leads a battalion of five thousand commoners and soldiers coming under the command of the vanguard Niu He to take Mao'erling. Niu He underestimates the enemy's strength, and his camp is raided during a nighttime sortie led by the bandit leader Gaixiong, which results in great losses. Luckily, Mulan comes to Niu He's aid with her troops, and she also manages to take Xishan through a stratagem. Niu He, to conceal the losses suffered by his army, does not reward Mulan for her achievement. He Rugu and others are indignant at this injustice, but Mulan manages to appease them using a trick.

The generalissimo Xin Ping personally visits the place where the camp is located. Niu He falsely reports that the military plans have been leaked. He slanders Mulan as intractable and refractory. Mulan, seeing that the generalissimo does not mention her military accomplishments, knows that Niu He is envious of her ability and sagacity and secretly sighs over her sad fate.

The generalissimo Xin Ping personally visits the strategic location occupied by the bandits and investigates their stronghold. He manages to capture Gaixiong and to take Gao Pass from the enemy with a stratagem. The bandit leader of Xiaohong Mountain, Zhao Rang, is set on avenging Gaixiong. He goes to battle against the Wei army with his female cousin Lu Wanhua but is defeated every time by Mulan.

The army supervisor Sun Siqiao concentrates solely on defending his position, always refusing to attack. Thus, six years pass by without the slightest progress. The Wei ruler issues an order urging Xin Ping to advance the army. Xin Ping consults with all the generals on how to proceed. Niu He suggests the stratagem of offering amnesty and recommends sending Hua Hu as emissary; in fact, his true intention is to "kill with a borrowed sword." Xin Ping therefore promotes Mulan as assistant commander and acting vice general in charge of carrying the amnesty proclamation. Sun Siqiao keeps her as a hostage and orders Zhao Rang to give his cousin Lu Wanhua to Hua Hu as a concubine in order to keep him at bay. Mulan has no choice but to agree for the sake of expediency, but eventually her secret is discovered by Lu Wanhua. Mulan declares her true feelings, and Lu Wanhua, who had long harbored the intention of returning to the Chinese side, expresses her willingness to surrender to the Northern Wei. The two girls become sworn sisters and make a vow to both marry Wang. With a stratagem, Lu Wanhua lets Mulan escape from the bandits' mountain stronghold. She also works to sabotage from within Zhao Rang's plan to feign surrender, and as a result Zhao Rang is killed by firearms. When the Xiaohong Mountain stronghold is taken, Sun Siqiao is captured and killed. Lu Wanhua takes this chance to seek refuge among the bandit lairs of Black Mountain in order to act as a mole. Mulan is hit in the course of the battle, and she spits blood; she remains at Xiaohong Mountain to recover.

Xin Ping personally leads the campaign against Black Mountain. The bandit leader's wife Miao Fengxian has extremely lethal flying cymbals, with which she kills Niu He at the foot of his horse and injures many high generals. Xin Ping is left at his wit's end. Mulan, who has by now recovered from her injuries, is able to counter the flying cymbals with the magic arrow given to her by Li Jing, the heavenly king who bears the pagoda [in his hand]. As a result, Miao Fengxian is stabbed to death. He Hu crosses the Black River and flees. Xin Ping appoints Hua Hu as vanguard to chase after him. Mulan crosses the Black River by means of a wine jug and goes straight to Black Mountain.

Since Xin Ping has not been able to quell the bandits for seven years, the Wei ruler plans to dispatch an army supervisor to urge the advance of the army. Following Wulühe's advice, he orders examinations in order to recruit new officials. Wang Qingyun places first with great honors, and he is sent as army supervisor. When Mulan and Wang Qingyun meet, they both are bashful. Wang Qingyun observes the topographical configuration of Black Mountain, and he writes a memorial to ask that the "red coat big cannon" be sent in order to attack the enemy. These weapons take over two years to be manufactured in the arsenal of the Ministry of War. As soon as they are completed, they are immediately sent to Black River. Twelve years have already passed since Mulan joined the army. Black Mountain is bombarded, and He Hu flees for his life, but Mulan manages to capture him, while Lu Wanhua leads the bandits to surrender.

Hua Mulan calls back her troops and, together with Mo Qianzhu and He Rugu, returns to her hometown, where she is reunited with her family. Mulan takes off her military garments and resumes her feminine appearance. When she comes out to meet Mo and He, the two are awestruck. The story is immediately spread across the whole of Pingyang. When it reaches the ears of the Wei emperor, he summons Mulan to court. Mulan has joined the army in place of her father, fighting outside of the Great Wall for twelve years, and while doing so she has not only remained loyal and filial, but she has also managed to return with her chastity intact. For all these reasons, Mulan can truly be considered the foremost hero among women. Thereupon, she is granted the title of "chaste and filial lady of first rank." Lu Wanhua is granted the title of "loyal and righteous lady." Wang Qingyun is appointed minister of personnel. A date is chosen, and the wedding is celebrated.

Zhongguo tongsu xiaoshuo zongmu tiyao, 1990, pp. 699–700.

Translated by Maria Franca Sibau

BIBLIOGRAPHY

A Ying 阿英, comp. *Wan Qing wenxue congchao: Shuochang wenxue juan* 晚清文學叢鈔。說唱文學卷. Vol. 2. Beijing: Zhonghua shuju, 1959.

Ahern, Emily M. "The Power and Pollution of Chinese Women." In *Women in Chinese Society*, edited by Margery Wolf and Roxane Witke, 193–214. Stanford, CA: Stanford University Press, 1975.

Allen, Joseph R. "Dressing and Undressing the Chinese Warrior." *Positions* 4, no. 2 (1996): 343–50.

Besio, Kimberly. "Gender, Loyalty, and the Reproduction of the Wang Zhaojun Legend: Some Social Ramifications of Drama in the Late Ming." *Journal of the Economic and Social History of the Orient* 40, no. 2 (1997): 251–82.

Carlitz, Katherine. "Desire, Danger, and the Body: Stories of Women's Virtue in Late Ming China." In *Engendering China: Women, Culture, and the State*, edited by Gail Hershatter, Christina K. Gilmartin, Lisa Rofel, and Tyrene White, 101–24. Cambridge, MA: Harvard University Press, 1994.

Chang, Tai-hung. *War and Popular Culture: Resistance in Modern China, 1937–1945*. Berkeley: University of California Press, 1994.

Chen, Fan Pen. "Female Warriors, Magic, and the Supernatural in Traditional Chinese Novels." In *The Annual Review of Women in World Religions*, edited by Arvind Sharma and Katerine K. Young, vol. 2, pp. 93–109. Albany: State University of New York Press, 1991.

Chen Fang 陳方. *Xu Wei ji qi "Sisheng yuan" yanjiu* 徐渭及其《四聲猿》研究. Hong Kong: Hongda chubanshe, 2002.

Chen, Sanping. "From Mulan to Unicorn." *Journal of Asian History* 39, no. 1 (2005): 23–43.

Chin, Frank. "Come All Ye Asian American Writers of the Real and the Fake." In *Aiiieeeee! An Anthology of Chinese American and Japanese American Literature*, edited by Jeffrey Paul Chan et al., 1–92. New York: Meridian, 1991.

Chu Renhuo 褚人穫. *Sui Tang yanyi* 隋唐演義. Taipei: Shijie shuju, 1962.

Cole, Alan. *Mothers and Sons in Chinese Buddhism*. Stanford, CA: Stanford University Press, 1998.

Dong Jian 董健, ed. *Zhongguo xiandai xiju zongmu tiyao* 中國現代戲劇總目提要. Nanjing: Nanjing daxue chubanshe, 2003.

Edwards, Louise. "Women Warriors and Amazons of the Mid Qing Texts *Jinghua yuan* and *Honglou meng*." *Modern Asian Studies* 29, no. 2 (1995): 225–55.

———. "Re-fashioning the Warrior Hua Mulan: Changing Norms of Sexuality in China." *IIAS Newsletter* 48 (Summer 2008): 6–7.

Fu, Poshek. *Between Shanghai and Hong Kong: The Politics of Chinese Cinemas*. Stanford, CA: Stanford University Press, 2003.

Goldstein, Joshua. "Mei Lanfang and the Nationalization of the Peking Opera, 1912–1930." *Positions* 7, no. 2 (1999): 377–420.

———. *Drama Kings: Players and Public in the Re-creation of Peking Opera, 1870–1937*. Berkeley: University of California Press, 2007.

Hsiung, Anne-Marie. "A Feminist Re-vision of Xu Wei's Ci Mulan and Nü Zhuangyuan." In *China in a Polycentric World: Essays in Chinese Comparative Literature*, edited by Yingjin Zhang, 73–89. Stanford, CA: Stanford University Press, 1999.

Huang, Martin. *Negotiating Masculinities in Late Imperial China*. Honolulu: University of Hawai'i Press, 2006.

Hung, Chang-tai. "Female Symbols of Resistance in Chinese Wartime Spoken Drama." *Modern China* 15, no. 2 (1989): 149–77.

———. *War and Popular Culture: Resistance in Modern China, 1937–1945*. Berkeley: University of California Press, 1994.

Idema, Wilt. "Female Talent and Female Virtue: Xu Wei's *Nü Zhuangyuan* and Meng Chengshun's *Zhenwen ji*." In *Ming Qing xiqu guoji yantaohui wenji* 明清戲曲國際研討會論文集, edited by Hua Wei 華瑋 and Wang Ailing 王璦玲, 549–71. Taipei: Zhongyang yanjiuyuan, 1998.

———. "Evil Parents and Filial Offspring: Some Comments on the *Xiangshan baojuan* and Related Texts." *Studies in Central and East Asian Religions* 12, no. 1 (2001): 41–93.

Idema, Wilt, and Beata Grant. *The Red Brush: Writing Women of Imperial China*. Cambridge, MA: Harvard University Press, 2004.

Jiang, Jin. *Women Playing Men: Yue Opera and Social Change in Twentieth-Century Shanghai*. Seattle: University of Washington Press, 2009.

Judge, Joan. *The Precious Raft of History: The Past, the West, and the Woman Question in China*. Stanford, CA: Stanford University Press, 2008.

Kaulbach, Barbara M. "The Woman Warrior in Chinese Opera: An Image of Reality or Fiction?" Translated by Christian Rogowski. *Fu Jen Studies* 15 (1982): 69–82.

Kingston, Maxine Hong. *The Woman Warrior: Memoir of a Girlhood among Ghosts.* New York: Knopf, 1976.

Ko, Dorothy. *Teachers of the Inner Chambers: Women and Culture in Seventeenth-Century China.* Stanford, CA: Stanford University Press, 1994.

———. *Every Step a Lotus: Shoes for Bound Feet.* Berkeley: University of California Press, 2001.

———. *Cinderella's Sisters: A Revisionist History of Footbinding.* Berkeley: University of California Press, 2005.

Kwa, Shiamin. "Songs of Ourselves: Xu Wei's (1521–1593) *Four Cries of a Gibbon (Sisheng yuan).*" Ph.D. diss., Harvard University, Cambridge, MA, 2008.

Lan, Feng. "The Female Individual and the Empire: A Historicist Approach to Mulan and Kingston's Woman Warrior." *Comparative Literature* 55, no. 3 (2003): 235–6.

Lee, Jeanne M. *The Song of Mulan.* Arden, NC: Front Street, 1995.

Li Liuyi 李六乙. *Hua Mulan* 花木蘭 [Script]. Beijing: Li Liuyi xiju gongzuo she, 2008.

Li, Siu Leung. *Cross-Dressing in Chinese Opera.* Hong Kong: Hong Kong University Press, 2007.

Li Xiusheng 李修生. *Guben xiqu jumu tiyao* 古本戲曲劇目提要. Beijing: Wenhua yishu chubanshe, 1997.

Li Zhongming 李仲明 and Tan Xiuying 譚秀英. *Mei Lanfang* 梅蘭芳. Shijiazhuang: Hebei jiaoyu chubanshe, 2001.

Liang Yicheng 梁一成. *Xu Wei di wenxue yu yishu* 徐渭的文學與藝術. Taipei: Yiwen yinshuguan, 1976.

Luo Yuming 羅玉明. *Zhongguo wenxue shi* 中國文學史. Shanghai: Fudan daxue chubanshe, 1996.

Ma, Qian, trans. "Mulan." In *Women in Traditional Chinese Theater: The Heroine's Play,* edited by Qian Ma, 129–51. Lanham, MD: University Press of America, 2005.

McMahon, Keith. *Misers, Shrews, and Polygamists: Sexuality and Male-Female Relations in Eighteenth-Century Chinese Fiction.* Durham, NC: Duke University Press, 1994.

Nio Joe Lan. *Hua Mu-Lan: Een studie en een der Mu-Lan-verhalen*. Batavia: China Instituut, 1939.

Ouyang Yuqian 歐陽予倩. "Mulan congjun 木蘭從軍." *Wenxian* 文獻 6 (1939): 1–31.

———. *Ouyang Yuqian wenji* 歐陽予倩文集. Beijing: Zhongguo xiju chubanshe, 1980.

Owen, Stephen, trans. "The Ballad of Mu-Lan." In *Anthology of Chinese Literature*, Stephen Owen, 241. New York: Norton, 1996.

Theiss, Janet M. *Disgraceful Matters: The Politics of Chastity in Eighteenth-Century China*. Berkeley: University of California Press, 2004.

Wang Zheng. *Women of the Chinese Enlightenment: Oral and Textual Histories*. Berkeley: University of California Press, 1999.

Wei Yuanfu 韋元甫. "Mulan shi 木蘭詩." In *Yuefu shiji* 樂府詩集, 373–5. Beijing: Zhonghua shuju, 1979.

Wichmann, Elizabeth. *Listening to Theatre: The Aural Dimensions of Beijing Opera*. Honolulu: University of Hawai'i Press, 1991.

Wu Pei-yi. "Yang Miaozhen: A Woman Warrior in Thirteenth-Century China." *Nan Nü* 4, no. 2 (2002): 137–70.

Xu Shuofang 徐朔方. *Wan Ming qujia nianpu* 晚明曲家年譜. Vol. 2. Hangzhou: Zhejiang guji chubanshe, 1993.

Xu Wei 徐渭. *Sisheng yuan, gedai xiao (fu)* 四聲猿歌代嘯付. Edited by Zhou Zhongming 周中明. Shanghai: Shanghai guji chubanshe, 1984.

Xu Zifang 徐子方. *Ming zaju shi* 明雜劇史. Beijing: Zhonghua shuju, 2003.

Yan Quanyi 顏全毅. *Qingdai jingju wenxue shi* 清代京劇文學史. Beijing: Beijing chubanshe, 2005.

Zeng Bairong 曾白融, ed. *Jingju jumu cidian* 京劇劇目詞典. Beijing: Zhongguo xiju chubanshe, 1989.

Zhang Shaoxian 張紹賢. *Beiwei qishi guixiao liezhuan* 北魏奇史閨孝烈傳. In *Guben xiaoshuo jicheng*. Shanghai: Shanghai guji chubanshe, 1990.

Zhongguo jingju shi, shang juan 中國京劇史，上卷. Beijing: Zhongguo xiju chubanshe, 2005.

Zhongguo tongsu xiaoshuo zongmu tiyao 中國通俗小說總目提要. Beijing: Zhongguo wenlian chubanshe, 1990.

Zhongxiao yonglie qinü zhuan 忠孝勇烈奇女傳. In *Guben xiaoshuo jicheng* 古本小說集成. Shanghai: Shanghai guji chubanshe, 1990.

Zhou Yibai 周貽白. *Mingren zaju xuan* 明人雜劇選. Beijing: Renmin chubanshe, 1985.

Zuo Pengjun 左鵬軍. *Wan Qing minguo chuanqi zaju kaosuo* 晚清民國傳奇雜劇考索. Beijing: Renmin wenxue chubanshe, 2005.

GLOSSARY

A

An Lushan 安祿山

B

Beiwei qishi guixiao liezhuan 北魏奇史閨孝烈傳
Bu Wancang 卜萬蒼

C

Chang'e 嫦哦
Chen Xu 陳栩
Chen Yunshang 陳雲裳
Cheng Yaojin 程咬金
chou 丑
Chu 楚
Chu Renhuo 褚人穫
Chu Suiliang 褚遂良
chuanqi 傳奇
Ci Mulan tifu congjun 雌木蘭替父從軍
Congjun daoshang 從軍道上
cuan 攛

D

Daifu zheng 代父征
dan 旦
Dianjiangchun 點降唇
Dou Jiande 竇建德
Dou Xianniang 竇線娘

F

Fang Xuanling 房玄齡

G

Guanyin 觀音
Guiju 桂劇
Gujin yuelü 古今樂錄
Guo Maoqian 郭茂倩

H
Han 漢
Han Xin 韓信
Heshana Khan 曷娑那可汗
Hetian 和田
Hua Hu 花弧
Hua Mulan 花木蘭
huadan 花旦
Hunjianglong 混江龍
Huo Qubing 霍去病

J
jingang 金剛
Jishengcao 寄生草

L
lao 老
Li Jing 李靖
Li Liuyi 李六乙
Liang Shanbo 梁山伯
Liu Bang (Han Gaozu) 劉邦（漢高祖）
Liu Wuzhou 劉武周
Liu Yuandu 柳元度
Loulan 樓蘭

M
manzi 蠻子
Mei Lanfang 梅蘭芳
Meng Jiangnü 孟姜女
Meng Jiao 孟郊
Mulan congjun 木蘭從軍
Mulan qinü quanzhuan 木蘭奇女全傳
Mulan qinü zhuan 木蘭奇女傳
Mulan shi 木蘭詩
Munan 木難

N
Nezhaling 那吒令

O
Ouyang Yuqian 歐陽予倩

P
Pifu 丕夫

Q
Qi Rushan 齊如山
Qin Shubao 秦叔寶
Qin Xiu 秦休
Qingjiang yin 清江引
Qiu Jin 秋瑾
Queta zhi 鵲踏枝

S
Shan Xiongxin 單雄信
Shi Siming 史思明
Shua haier 耍孩兒
Shuangtu ji 雙兔記
Sisheng yuan 四聲猿
Sui Tang yanyi 隋唐演義
Sun Quan 孫權
suona 嗩吶

T
Tang Taizong 唐太宗
Tianxiale 天下樂
tie 貼
Tiele 鐵勒
Tiying 緹縈
Tujue 突厥
Tuoba 拓跋

W
wai 外
Wang Shichong 王世充
Wang Wei 王維
Wang Xizhi 王羲之
Wei 魏
Wei Qing 衛青
Wei Yuanfu 韋元甫
Wei Zheng 魏徵

X
Xianbei 鮮卑
Xiang Yu 項羽
Xiao Shi 蕭史
Xiaohuan 小鬟
xiaosheng 小生

Xin Mulan congjun 新木蘭從軍
Xin Ping 辛平
Xinhua Film Company 新華影業公司
Xiongnu 匈奴
Xu Shiji 徐世勣
Xu Wei 徐渭
Xue Rengui 薛仁貴

Y
Yang Su 楊素
Yao'er 咬兒
Yin Ci 殷慈
Yiyuan sizhong 漪園四種
Yong'en 永恩
Youhulu 油葫蘆
Youzi yin 遊子吟
Yuchi Gong 尉遲恭
Yue Fei 岳飛
Yue opera (Cantonese) 粵劇
Yue opera (Zhejiang) 越劇
yuefu 樂府
Yuefu shiji 樂府詩集
Yuwen Huaji 宇文化及

Z
zaju 雜劇
Zaqu geci 雜曲歌詞
Zhang Liang (Zifang) 張良 (子房)
Zhang Shankun 善琨
Zhang Shaoxian 張紹賢
Zhang Xu 章須
Zhongxiao yonglie Mulan zhuan 忠孝勇烈木蘭傳
Zhu Yingtai 祝英台